D1398660

CALL ME ADNAN

ALSO BY REEM FARUQI

Anisa's International Day

Golden Girl

Unsettled

Amira's Picture Day

Lailah's Lunchbox

I Can Help

Milloo's Mind

CALL ME ADNAN

Reem Faruqi

HARPER

An Imprint of HarperCollinsPublishers

Call Me Adnan
Copyright © 2023 by Reem Faruqi
All rights reserved. Printed in the United States of America.
No part of this book may be used or reproduced in any manner
whatsoever without written permission except in the case of
brief quotations embodied in critical articles and reviews. For
information address HarperCollins Children's Books, a division of
HarperCollins Publishers, 195 Broadway, New York, NY 10007.
www.harpercollinschildrens.com

Library of Congress Cataloging-in-Publication Data
Names: Faruqi, Reem, author.
Title: Call me Adnan / Reem Faruqi.
Description: First edition. | New York : Harper, [2023] | Audience: Ages
    8–12. | Audience: Grades 4–6. | Summary: Twelve-year-old Adnan
    dreams of making it to the Ultimate Table Tennis championship, but
    when tragedy strikes his family, Adnan loses his passion for table tennis
    and must learn to channel his grief and heal.
Identifiers: LCCN 2022045238 | ISBN 978-0-06-328494-4 (hardcover)
Subjects: CYAC: Novels in verse. | Grief—Fiction. | Family life—
    Fiction. | Table tennis—Fiction. | Pakistani Americans—Fiction. |
    LCGFT: Novels in verse. | Novels.
Classification: LCC PZ7.5.F37 Cal 2023 | DDC [Fic]—dc23
LC record available at https://lccn.loc.gov/2022045238

Typography by Carla Weise
23 24 25 26 27 LBC 5 4 3 2 1
First Edition

For my brothers, Osman, Talha, and Hamzah, and
my uncle Jim, who are always there for me and who
make the table tennis ball f l y . . .

and Nana for sharing Yusuf's legacy

PART 1

Thrust
Thrust is a force
that pushes an
airplane forward.

The Beginning

Rumor has it
when I was small,
if I would lose
I would hide under the table tennis table.
But now I'm not small.
And more importantly
I don't lose.

Table Tennis

Something
I'm good at.
Really good at.

You would think
on a small table
I wouldn't get tired,
but at the end of the game
my legs are wobbly
my arms stretchy
my face sweaty.

Magic Trick

When I was little,
maybe my brother Rizwan's age
(he's two and a half years old),
my father, Abu, showed me backspin.
He sliced the paddle under the ball,
added enough spin
so the ball would bounce bounce bounce toward me.
I'd reach my fingers out
but then
the ball would suddenly

       u   r

t   n

and bounce right back to him.

Magic!

My Trick Now That I'm Twelve

When I serve,
I toss the ball up,
hold the paddle flat,
brush underneath the ball,
adding the perfect touch of spin.
So when the opponent
tries to get the ball,
it'll spin

the

        opposite

                direction.

    Success!

Why I Like Winning

My favorite part of Coca-Cola
is opening a fresh new can,
pulling the silver tab up.
The pop of success,
the sizzle of ice cubes
when Coke meets ice,
watching the fizz bubble up high.
I always drink the fizz right up.

The first time
I won,
I couldn't wait to win
again.

I felt like Coca-Cola fizz.

Winning is like being thirsty for
Coca-Cola,

I'll always want

more.

Me

I'm not really tall
for a twelve-year-old,
more on the small side.
So I look like a ten-year-old,
even though I eat *a lot* of
pasta, popcorn, pizza, Pringles, pretzels, parathas,
(Amma calls me Mr. P)
it doesn't really do
much.

I'm okay
at basketball but
would never try out
for the team.

Something cool about table tennis
is that the players
are all different sizes
different shapes.
All that matters is
how you hit the ball.

I'm Color-Blind

It means that
for me—

Orange is green.
Green is brown.
Blue is purple.
Purple is blue.

I like the two sides of my paddle,
one red,
one black.
It makes it easy
not to get confused.

My Mistakes

At first I thought the table tennis table
was brown,
until my big sister, Aaliyah,
laughed at me,
said *It's green*,
duh.

In kindergarten,
my parents realized I was color-blind.
When everyone painted self-portraits,
my face was green.
Everyone else's:
peaches and browns.

Oops.

When you make a mistake
and you can't even *see* the right answer,
it's not fair,
but Aaliyah doesn't care.
Now, Aaliyah likes to point at things
and asks me the colors,
laughs when I get them wrong.

I know that grass is green.
Duh.
But when she wears a shirt that's purple
and I say blue,
and my little brother, Riz, says puw-pul,
she laughs the laugh
that makes my eyebrows zip together
my skin hot.

Aaliyah rolls her eyes,
pats me on the head,
and says,
Good try!
Then rumples Riz's hair
and says,
Even though you're ten years younger
than your brother,
you're MUCH smarter.

I clench my fists tight,
like I'm holding my table tennis paddle,
and squeeze.

I don't like making mistakes.

It's Not Just Me

My uncle Zia is color-blind too,
but he paints
pieces of art.
Swirly calligraphy,
mixed-up colors everywhere
that people buy
for lots of money.
And whenever I tell Aaliyah that
and point to Zia Mamu's art,
Aaliyah says,
That would help you
if you knew how
to hold a paintbrush.
But you can't even hold a pencil properly!

Left-Handed

I am
left-handed
which Amma says
means I'm more creative.
But my teacher Ms. Morgan
says my writing is chicken scratch.

Zia Mamu is lucky he can paint.
But I'm lucky too:
in table tennis I'm ambidextrous—
I can play
      and win
           using **both** hands.
        Whether the paddle is in my
left hand

                                   or right
                                   hand

I can smash the ball
D
O
W
N

on the very edge of the table,
getting the ball in.

Aaliyah's too scared to try me!

Famous Left-Handed People

Barack Obama
Einstein
Pelé
Aristotle
Wasim Akram
Tom Cruise
Brad Pitt
Leonardo da Vinci
Bart Simpson too!

Aviation Alphabet

Even though
my big sister Aaliyah's writing is better than mine
and she's always reading,
and acts smarter than me,
there's something I know
more than her,
way more:
every single letter in the aviation alphabet.

When Aaliyah tries,
she makes mistakes,
but I never do.

My Name in Aviation Alphabet

Alfa
Delta
November
Alfa
November

Zulu
Alfa
Kilo
India
Romeo

These words that
not everyone knows
make up my name,
making it special
to me.

Amma works in the aviation industry
She made a   l   o   n   g
road trip
short,
when she taught me the aviation alphabet.

It's like our secret code.

My Name Is

Adnan Zakir
(no middle name!)
Sometimes
Amma and Abu
call me *Dani*,
but I tell them,
Call me Adnan!
I like my name
just the way it is.
Alfa **D**elta **N**ovember **A**lfa **N**ovember

Me

The coolest thing
about my name
is that when the teacher
goes in alphabetic order,
my place in line changes
with my name.
If they go by my last name, Zakir,

(for book reports),
I'm last.
If they go by my first name, Adnan,
(for PE),
I'm first.
I wish I got to choose.

My Best Friend, Sufian

Is one year older than me
and makes sure *I* know it.

His little sister, Summar, is one month younger than me.
I make sure *she* knows it.

Sufian was my neighbor first
but then became my best friend.
Sufian lives on the top of the hill
and when his ball rolled   d

                              o

                                      w

                                          n

                                              the

                                              hill,

landed in my driveway,
he ended up staying,
passing the ball back and forth
every day onward.

He wanted to swap Summar with me
when we were little,
give Summar to Aaliyah,
take me instead.
But our parents just laughed,
said no.

Even though Sufian is my best friend,
once in a while, I feel closer to Summar.
And not just because I'm closer to her in age
or that we're in the same grade,
but I'm not going to tell Sufian
or Summar
(obviously).

How It Started

A table tennis table
was donated,
placed
in the corner
of the masjid.
In between the water coolers
and the stacks of shoes,
I started hitting balls back and forth,
back and forth.

When I got better,
started beating the uncles
started getting compliments
started drawing a crowd
(Summar even).
Abu asked me if
I wanted to learn more—
get a coach,
start training,
compete in tournaments.
I didn't even need to think before I said
YES.

I didn't even know that was an option,
that there were competitions
for people in Atlanta,

for people just like me.

Who I Usually Play Against

Abu
Sufian
Aaliyah
Uncles from the masjid
Friends
People I usually know
and Summar.

Summar

My best friend Sufian's sister
used to be really annoying.
Now Summar is not so bad.

Whether I call her
Hey, Winter!
Hey, Spring!
Hey, Autumn!
Summer always turns around.

What I Like about Summer

She knows how to play table tennis
better than all the other girls
even some boys
and even though I beat her
every time,
sometimes she gets the tiniest bit
close.

But Summer could beat me in basketball
most times
so I guess we're even.

When Sufian Smiles

His eyes get really small.

Sufian squint smiles
when the Atlanta Hawks
score a winning three-pointer
in the fourth quarter.

Sufian squint smiles
after he sips the mango lassi
he blended together
with the right amount of sweetness.

Sufian squint smiles
when he makes the perfect
swish of ball
meeting net
and air.
(This happens a lot!)

When Summar Smiles

Her eyes don't squint like Sufian
but stay the same size.

When Summar smiles,
her nose scrunches,
making her face
better than before.

When I Grow Up

I want to be a professional table tennis player
or a pilot,
so I watch airplane videos
filmed from the cockpit
and play Pilot Pro video games with Sufian.
We give Riz an extra video game controller
but turn it off,
so he thinks he's playing with us
but he's not.

When Sufian Grows Up

He wants to be a chef.
He watches the *Kid Chefs Championship*
on the Food Network
over and over.

After school, at Sufian's house
I watch him practice.

I don't like eggs
but Sufian's eggs
are different.

He cooks creamy eggs,
adding butter,
milk,
salt,
and cooks it a special way,
taking the pan off the stove
and putting it back on.

He fries fluffy pakoras
and cooks keema,
filling spring rolls
in neat cylinders.

He sautés leaves of spinach,
melting them with golden turmeric,
and serves it onto swollen rice.

He folds samosa pastry
into bite-sized triangles
and serves them all times of the year,
not just Ramadan.

Sufian's mom, Mariam Aunty,
lets him cook,
but tells him over and over
CLEAN UP AS YOU COOK!

Only thing is,
Sufian is messy.
Very Messy.
And doesn't clean until the very end.

So when I film videos of him cooking
(he always shares what he has with me),
he asks me to help him clean up.

With a full stomach,
I don't mind.

When Summar Grows Up

Summar collects dead bugs,
        velvety bees,
        shimmery dragonflies,
        cottony moths,
        even crispy roaches,
in a plastic box
lined with paper towels.

Tells us that when she's an adult
she's going to be an entomologist,
a scientist who studies bugs.

At Summar's birthday party,
she gave out goody bags
with shiny insect stickers.

When Summar sees a dead bug at school,
she'll put it in her lunch box pocket,
to add to her bug collection.
But sometimes she forgets to tell her mom.
Mariam Aunty unzips Summar's lunch box
and screams.
She hates when Summar does that.

When My Siblings Grow Up

I bet Riz will want to work with airplanes
because every time he sees a plane,
or hears one,
he stops what he's doing,
runs to the window,
points up.

Maybe we can be copilots.

Aaliyah wants to be a teacher,
which isn't very exciting
if you ask me.

Why would you want to go back to school
when you're finally done with it?

Before: Playing Table Tennis
When I Was Eight Years Old

In table tennis,
Aaliyah doesn't care
if she wins or loses,
which I will never understand.
But at least she plays with me.

When we were little
and Amma and Abu were napping,
Aaliyah and I would whip the tablecloth off the table
and line up chapter books
on the dining table to make a net.
Sometimes the books would   w   b   l
                                                    o   b   e

and   t
              o
                        p
                             p
                                  l
                                        e,

and Amma would scold us
when she would see the tablecloth
crumpled in a corner,
but that didn't stop us.

After: Playing Table Tennis
When I Was Eleven Years Old

A knock on the door
and a ring of the bell—

a **BIG** brown box
with MY name on it,
(Aaliyah's too).

. . .

My heart beat fast, and we ripped open the package:
a brand-new table tennis table!

I don't usually high-five Aaliyah,
but that time we did.

Magic Trick (Now That I'm Twelve)

I take Riz's fat fingers
(he has dimples for knuckles),
wrap them around the paddle,
and show him how to hit the ball.

Riz can barely see over the table—
swings the paddle,
misses a lot,
but I cheer when he hits the ball back.

Riz shrieks with joy.
when I do the trick—
make the ball bounce
right back to me with spin.
Rizzie laughs the loudest.
Table tennis is magic.

Why I Love Table Tennis

It's like tennis
except smaller
and faster
(like me).

I love hitting something so tiny
and having power
over the ball.

In table tennis,
a flick of the wrist
changes direction.

Adding spin
making the ball move

                           here

there

              everywhere.

My Favorite Sound

The ball
tap tapping
spin spinning
back and forth
clears my mind.

When my paddle's in my hand,
the only thing I have to worry about
is thrusting the ball back
across the net.
I focus on my half of the green table
(although to me it looks brown!).

I love twirling my paddle,
while I wait between serves.

When I play,
people stop
what they're doing
to watch.

With table tennis,
it doesn't matter
if you're as young as Rizwan,

or as old as Dadi,
you can join right in.

It doesn't matter
if I'm small
or skinny,
or twelve.
With a paddle in my hand,
I become important.

How I Discovered Table Tennis

I kept looking for *my* sport
soccer
swimming
basketball
(Sufian's sport obviously)
but for me
when I picked up the paddle
I was good at returning the ball
and I was quick.

I felt Relief
mixed with Excitement
to be good at something,

and the more I play,
the better I get.

When I play table tennis,
my feet feel light
floaty
and I can play all day
never get tired.

I love being in control—
playing a sport I like
makes me keep coming back
for more.

When I play basketball or soccer,
I don't stand out
on the field
or the court.

But when I'm playing table tennis,
just me
against my opponent
and I'm scoring all the points,
I become the star.

Talent

Coach Khalil
is the best table tennis coach
in our area.
We book a session
for thirty minutes.
Abu's really excited,
tells me I'll get even better
when I play people who are better than me.
But Amma's mouth twists
when she hears how much it costs,
puts her hand on her belly.

Coach Khalil tells Abu
I have talent and potential.

Usually when I'm told
I have
potential,
on a report card or a progress report,
I don't care.

But this time,
I do.

Coach Khalil Says

It's a good idea to know the terminology,
so you can get even better.

You mean
crush your opponent
and make them lose?

The lines by Coach Khalil's eyes
deepen into a W.
Coach Khalil doesn't smile,
but the corners of his mouth
t-w-i-t-c-h
before he answers,

Exactly.

Game of Spin

Coach Khalil says,
Table tennis is a game of spin.
To understand the strokes,
you have to understand
each type of spin.

Want to hit the ball harder?

I nod.

If you learn topspin well, you can do that.

If you want to get better,
you must learn how to use spin
to your advantage,
how to disguise it,
and how to play against it.

If I understand more,
I can win more.

This I understand.

Favorite Snack

Popcorn.

The best is when it's all buttery
movie style—
I don't even need a movie to watch.

I love dipping my fingers
into the buttery goo
at the bottom of the crumply bag
and crunching on unpopped kernels.

If a day goes by
when I don't eat popcorn,
my day feels like I'm missing something.

Popcorn Feet

By the table tennis table,
my feet are like kernels
Popping

Moving
Tapping
Jumping
They don't stop until I win.

If a day goes by
when I don't play table tennis,
my day feels like I'm missing something.

Rice Krispies

Whenever Abu pours a bowl of his favorite cereal with
    milk,
Rice Krispies
(mine is Cinnamon Toast Crunch),
Abu tells everyone to quiet down.
Abu leans his ear next to his cereal bowl.
Do you hear that?

Snap!
    Crackle!
        Pop!

Snap! Crackle! Pop!

Abu watches me play table tennis,
says I'm like the Rice Krispies slogan

Snap . . .
my arms back.
Crackle . . .
move my paddle forward.
Pop . . .
the ball into its corner.

Whenever I score a point,
a really good one
Abu high-fives me
snaps his fingers
whoops

Snap!
      Crackle!
            Pop!

Abu's Advice

When I practice with Abu,
we volley the ball

                y
       l
f
let it back and forth.

In table tennis
you can't hit the ball too hard
at the wrong angle
otherwise it'll go too far
miss the table.

You can't hit the ball too soft
at the wrong angle
otherwise it won't go over the net.

You have to know when and how hard
to hit the ball
to win.

When Abu challenges me to a match,
I'm close
but I lose
my shoulders slump.

I can't lose.

Losing makes me feel awful.
Losing makes me want
to hide under the table
to *never* feel this way
again.

Abu says,
It's okay! Table tennis should be fun!
Remember it's just a game!

Adults always say that.

Goals

Coach Khalil
gives me a piece of paper,
doesn't complain when my writing
is messy,
tells me to write down my goals.

My goals in table tennis:
Compete in as many tournaments as possible.
Make it to the biggest tournament ever, the Ultimate
    Table Tennis Championship.

When I practice,
sure, I'm there to have fun,

but

the second the match begins,
I'm not playing to have fun anymore.
I'm not playing to lose.
I'm here to win.

Coach Khalil nods
when he reads my paper.
He gets it.

My goals in life:
I think of Riz,
my little brother.
It doesn't matter if
he's good
or naughty,
his eyes shine
when he looks at me.

I want to be the best
Big brother.

My Family

(There are five of us.)
Abu is thirty-seven.
Amma is thirty-six.
Aaliyah is thirteen.
I'm twelve.
Riz is two.

But now Amma's tummy is growing.
She coos to her friends,
the aunties:

Aaliyah and Adnan
are so lucky
to have each other.
Riz is on his own.
But now he'll have a little friend too—
a little sister.
He'll get to be a big brother
inshallah!

I scoop up Riz
make a face at Aaliyah.
Doesn't matter what age we are,
us men need to stick together—got it?

Riz nods,
squeals as I thrust him high,
shrieks as I swoop him low,
turn him into
an airplane!

When I put him down,
Riz yells,
Again!
Again!

And you would think
it would be tiring

to swoop around a little brother
but I don't mind.

Vrooooom. Off we go . . .

If You Give a Ball . . .

Aaliyah:

> If you give her a ball of play dough,
> she will turn it into a perfect rose.

Sufian:

> If you give him a basketball,
> he will swoosh the ball in the net.

Summar:

> If you give her a gumball,
> she will blow a huge bubble.

Me:

> If you give me a table tennis ball and a paddle,
> I will challenge you to a match.

Aaliyah's Roses

Aaliyah takes Riz's play dough
shreds it into pieces
takes the smallest pieces
then the mediumest pieces
then the biggest pieces
curls them together
into a rose.

When Aaliyah's making a rose,
everything around her
goes
quiet.

That's what table tennis does for me too.

Aaliyah's Windowsill Bouquet

Aaliyah gives the rose to Amma
but Riz gets to it first
and smushes it in one go.

Aaliyah takes another ball of play dough
makes another rose
makes sure Amma gets it this time.

Amma coos every time:
So talented, Aaliyah!
She puts it on the windowsill
where more roses gather.

The play dough dries up
making the roses permanent
and perfect.

(I'd never tell her that though.)

Sufian's Mousse

Sufian breaks chocolate
melts it and melts butter too
whisks in egg yolks
beats egg whites into foam
pours in sugar,
vanilla, and heavy whipping cream
until he makes fluffy little mountains.
Sufian mixes it all together,
dividing it into cups,
then puts it in the fridge
serves it later.

The light, airy sweetness
invites me to eat
more and more.

When Sufian Bakes

When Sufian bakes,
it smells like melty sugar
and oozing cinnamon.

Sufian bakes
pastry rolls that flake
cinnamon rolls with loopy icing
chocolate bread in the shape of a star.

Riz says cinnamon like *si-man-im-in*.
You can always tell what Riz ate
by looking at his cheeks and chin,
nose too!

Riz's Favorite Rice Krispie Treats

Sufian wears his black apron
that says *MY KITCHEN IS HALAL*
that his dad, Zohair Uncle,
bought him.

The trick is you have to brown the butter,
says Sufian,
until it smells a little nutty
and the buttery bits are all brown
but not black!

Once it's brown,
Sufian melts in gelatin-free marshmallows
Rice Krispies
and a quarter teaspoon of sea salt.

Sufian flattens the sticky mix
slices it into sloppy squares
gives me almost all of it.

My mom's trying to be healthy . . .
Give it to Riz. It's his favorite.
Plus your dad is obsessed with

SNAP! CRACKLE! POP!

We yell at the same time.

Sufian's Experiments

Amma likes when I eat
new things with Sufian
so I'm not Mr. P anymore
(eating only pasta, popcorn, pizza, Pringles, pretzels,
    parathas).

Most of Sufian's things
are delicious
but sometimes
Sufian tries to be different,
pairs weird ingredients together
like eggs and grapes
and the food then is
GROSS.

Sufian

Sufian isn't into bugs
but is into squirrels.
On his bird feeder

he puts lunch leftovers
and even fancy crumbs of what he bakes.
Sufian's father, Zohair Uncle, shoos the squirrel
yells,
Get Out of Here!

What Sufian and I Google

I google

> Ghost serves (this is a serve with a lot of spin)
> The best table tennis athletes
> Smooth pilot landings

Sufian googles

> How to make a squirrel obstacle course
> Silicone baking mats
> How to make crème brûlée

Brothers

I wish I had a brother
who was closer to my age.
Sufian is my best friend
but he's still not a brother.

Idrees is
my other best friend,
      who is actually my cousin,
          who I also wish was my brother.

But he lives in Orchid, Florida,
(almost a two-hour drive from Universal Studios in
    Orlando!).
And I live in Atlanta, Georgia.

We see each other on holidays,
but that's not enough.

Far from it.

The Benefits of Four

Amma tells me,
With four children,
you can easily share:
—sticks of Kit Kat
—the walls of a room
—four sides of a board game

Amma's palms smooth her belly.
Inshallah, it'll be fun.

Laundry

Riz's favorite chore
is the laundry
(even though I do most of the work).
I pour a cup of blue detergent
hover him over the machine
while he splashes it in.

Abu loves to buy detergent
and yellow mango-ginger fragrance-booster beads

that make the clothes smell
even better.

I hover Riz again while he scatters the
beads in.

Then close the machine
let Riz sit on top
look down
to see the clothes dance
in bubbles of white.

My Job at Bedtime

Sometimes after Amma puts Riz in his crib
and Aaliyah's working on homework,
Abu's out of town,
Amma's doing the dishes.
And Riz is yelling and crying
instead of going to sleep.

Amma sighs,
looks around the room,
and turns to me.
Adnan, canyoupleasego?

Up the stairs,
Riz thrusts his blue bear and books through
the bars of his crib.

I ignore the bear and books.
It's a good thing
I'm small
and skinny too.
I climb right in
and hold him close,
listen as his big snuffles
turn to small sniffles.

And when he calls me Dani
it's okay,
I don't mind.

I put his head on my shoulder
his heartbeat to my heartbeat,
learn the language of his eyelashes
until he falls asleep.

Open close open close open close
Open   c l o s e
Open   c   l   o   s   e
Open   c   l   o   s   e   d.

My Family's Hair in Letters

My hair sticks up like the letter *l*
Aaliyah's hair waves into the letter *S*
When she's not wearing hijab, Amma's hair twists into
    the letter *Q*,
a big bun with a pencil in it.
Abu used to have hair like the letter *l*
but now his head looks more like the letter *O*, since
    he's bald.
Riz's hair curls into letter *c* all over his head.

My Family's Smiles

You can tell a lot about us
from our smiles.
Amma's smile starts tiny
gets big
takes four seconds
to reach her eyes.

Abu's bearded smile starts and stays medium.
Aaliyah's smile starts and stays big.

Rizzie's smile is always wide and open.
Me?
I smile when I need to.
More importantly, I smile when I play table tennis.

Coach Says

A natural high
is something you want to feel again
and again.
That's what table tennis
is like for him.

Abu chugs water
wipes sweat
says running is a natural high
that it makes him feel good.

For Amma, it's organizing
rows of hijabs and books
in rainbow colors.

For Aaliyah, it's music
that makes the room shake,
beats that make her feel like dancing.

For Riz, I think it's
pointing at airplanes
high in the sky.

For me, it was finally finding my sport, table tennis—
slicing the ball
and winning.

There's nothing like it.

Rally

When Abu's done with his run,
I challenge him to a match.

Before, Abu used to win
all of the time.
Now I win
most of the time.

Sometimes Abu and I
will stand   f   a   r
from the table to see
how long we can keep

the ball on the tiny table
in a big room.

Sometimes
when we have a long rally
and the ball is f l y i n g
back and forth,
from me to him
and him to me,
Amma will close her laptop.
She'll walk over to watch,
holding Rizzie back.
Aaliyah will put down her phone,
walk over to watch too.

Whether Abu wins the point
or me,
(Rizzie always cheers!)
table tennis hooks us in.
All in the room
around the table
together.

Rizwan

Round cheeks,
round belly,
his elbows
have little dimples you can poke.
His sticky hands have no knuckles,
just little dots.

His hair curls into *c*'s
and when you pull one gently
into a letter *l*
it'll bounce right back
into the letter *c*.

His hair is dark brown
but in the sunlight
it turns gold.
If you think his smile is big,
you have to see his eyes,
which get lots of compliments.
The cashier at the grocery store
says she wishes she had his l o n g eyelashes.
But I don't notice his eyelashes
just his eyes,
blinking happy circles that invite you closer.

When he wants me, he yells, *DANI! DANI!*
DANI!
at least three times
and I need to tell him, *Call me Adnan!*

He's the cutest baby in the world.

Except when he poops.

AIR PWANE!

Riz is obsessed with airplanes.
When I take him out in the backyard,
   to kick a ball
   blow bubbles
   draw with chalk

Everything stops
when a plane's overhead.

Riz will freeze
look up
shout,
AIR PWANE!
AIR PWANE!

One day when Amma's KitchenAid mixer was on,
whirring the sound of almost cookies,
Aaliyah was putting away flour,
and I was eating chocolate chips,
Abu heard the creak of the front door,
ran to look.
Riz was on the front lawn
pointing up.
AIR PWANE!
AIR PWANE!

Abu scooped him up.
You can't go outside alone!
Abu installed a child lock the next day,
rumpled Riz's curls,
squeezed his cheeks,
pretended to steal his nose,
told us,
Riz is something special.
But We Must Watch Out for Him!

Taking Riz to the Air Show

Abu's idea is to take all of us
to the air show.
Here, under cloudless skies,
planes zoom
every direction
even upside down,
my favorite.

Aaliyah's favorite
is when the planes release pink smoke
making a heart
and then another plane zooms through it
making an arrow.

I would gag
but the plane flying upside down
to make the heart
was pretty amazing.

Riz's favorite thing to do at the air show
is being scooped up high
and riding my shoulders.

On my shoulders,
Riz drums his hands
on my head
singing, *Dani* *Dani* *Dani!*

When we have the long walk back to the car,
I bring Riz down
hold him
and he must be tired
because he puts his head on my shoulder.
(Riz only does that when he's really tired.)

And then I feel his chest move
up
     down
          up
              down.

Riz is asleep!

Riz's Language

Gubble bum = bubble gum
Sgabetti = spaghetti
Chee kain = key chain
Brefkast = breakfast
Hod tog = hot dog
Jawwyfish = jellyfish
Air pwane = airplane

Riz's Places

Riz loves going to
the airport cell phone parking lot
the grocery store
the post office
and especially the masjid!

Imam Talha

Imam Talha
has a beard the color of a badger's tail
and a big smile to go with it—
welcomes us whenever we go to the masjid.

Imam Talha
has a voice that is loud
and when he leads us in prayer it echoes,
bounces around the hall.

Imam Talha
should be known by how he prays,
but instead
Riz and I know him by what he makes.

Imam Talha
knits and crochets
 chunky hats
 woolly sweaters
 thick shawls
 fuzzy socks
drives around Atlanta
passes it out to homeless people.

Whenever his trunk gets empty,
Imam Talha is quick to fill it again.

Imam Talha
crochets toys too,
like bunnies and bears,
stars and owls.

In Riz's crib
is his soft blue bear
with black eye buttons
that Imam Talha made.

Whenever Riz is close by.
Imam Talha
takes out his sock puppet.

Riz laughs and laughs.

If You Give a Ball . . .

If you give a fat ball of yarn to Imam Talha,
he will return it to you
as something totally different.

Downtime

When Imam Talha waits for the next prayer
and he's read his Quran already,
he starts reciting his morning and evening duas
takes out his knitting needles
or crochet hook
a fat ball of yarn
ignores the chuckles from the aunties
and gets to work.

When he sees Sufian and me looking,
he says,

Knitting helps me focus,
keeps my hands busy,
my mind calm.
You should try it!

> *Just like table tennis.*
> *Want to play?*

Imam Talha is surprisingly good!

Little Shadow

When Abu and Riz and I
go to the masjid on Friday,
Imam Talha booms his salam down at us.
He calls me Abu's Big Shadow
and calls Riz, Little Shadow.

Imam Talha says to call him I.T.
even though he doesn't work in I.T.
When I look at him funny,
he says, *Information Technology*
even though I do give some pretty good information
   around here . . .

Friday Jumuah Prayer

While Abu and I pray
Riz wobbles through the lines of men,
scooping up car keys.

Immediately after the prayer
I run to Riz
pry open his sweaty fingers
return the keys.
The men nod their thanks
while Imam Talha jokes,
Little Shadow has some expensive taste in cars!

Sunday School

Imam Talha teaches Sunday school,
gathers us together
for a community service project.

Imam Talha holds up a paper bag of little soap bars
tiny bottles of shampoos from Walmart
and socks he knitted.

Imam Talha lines us up into an assembly line
and we plop items into bags for homeless people.

Imam Talha labels and puts a donation box aside.
I'm also collecting more socks and blankets.
There's only so many I can make . . .

> *You could just buy them!*
> Sufian always says what he thinks.

I prefer to make mine—
it's from the heart.
Imam Talha taps his heart
smiles a bearded smile.
Plus, it's fun.
When all the bags are assembled,
Imam Talha booms, *GREAT JOB!*
Then he pretends to grate cheese
laughs loudly at his pun.
Then he asks, *Get it?*

Sufian and I roll our eyes.

Summar's Gifts

After Sunday school, when Sufian comes over
and Summar tags along,
I used to be annoyed.

Now I just act annoyed,
and I think Summar knows I'm playing.

Summar will bring over a toy car
or a toy plane,
and call Riz over for a magic trick
pretend to pull the toy out of his ear.

Riz loves it,
shrieks with joy,
runs into Summar's arms when she opens them
airplane wings wide.

Lucky Riz.

Bunny Poop

Whenever Summar wears her bunny hairband,
she pulls the ears up
brags how she's taller than me.

Some people say
I'm an excellent listener,
Summar brags,
tugging on her bunny ears.

My response is easy:
Did you know bunnies eat their own poop?
That always works.

Gross

When Summar walks,
she sometimes rattles
because she puts containers of gum
in her pocket.

Sometimes she has bubble gum tape
and sometimes wrapped-up rectangles of gum
and sometimes rattling cylinders of tiny rectangles.

Summar tells Riz,
I learned to blow a bubble
when I was two years old,
so you can too!

Don't give him gum, Summar!
intervenes Aaliyah.

Sufian adds,
Just because you knew how to blow a bubble
didn't mean you were very responsible!
Do you remember when you were little
and the wrong-colored gumball came out of the machine
you chewed it for a few seconds

and then put it back
into the machine
where the gumballs slide out?

GROSS!!!
Aaliyah and I yell
at the same time.

The Airport Cell Phone Lot

This is where we sometimes go for drives,
because Riz and I like to see planes
swoop high for takeoff
swoop low to land.

When I asked Amma how planes fly,
she said there are four stages of flight:
 Thrust forward
 Weight down
 Drag back
 Lift up

For a plane to soar,
it needs *all* those things to happen.

When I Soar

For me to soar
I play table tennis.

Thrust the ball forward.
Weight down on my foot.
Drag my arm back again.
Lift the ball over the net.

For me to soar in table tennis
I need all those things to happen.

If I don't play right
and I lose,
I feel smaller than I am—
insignificant.
I sink into failure
and the worst mood ever.

I'm not a pilot yet
but I can imagine
playing and winning in table tennis
feels like soaring in the skies.

How Aaliyah Soars

When she exercises
and the music turns on,
Aaliyah's always ready.
She doesn't skip a beat
doesn't miss a step
s t o p s what she's doing
s

       w

           a

                y

                     s

stomps
jumps
 . . . Zumba
 . . . Bollywood
 . . . rap

Aaliyah does it all.

Amma's Rules

When you memorize the thirtieth juz
of the Quran,
you get to go to
Universal Studios,
which is in Florida
where my favorite cousin,
Idrees, lives.

I complain about memorizing, but
sometimes I like the way
the Arabic words
glue together
into a melodious.
rhythm.
Don't tell Amma.

Rhythm

What Aaliyah has
when she reads Quran.
It's easy for her.
I've told Amma
how easy it is
for Aaliyah to memorize.
She reads it one time,
and in her memory
it goes,
never forgotten again.

Not fair.

Amma's Advice

Those who struggle
with the words of the Quran,
get more good deeds,
two times more.

"Verily the one who recites
the Quran beautifully,
smoothly,
precisely,
he'll be in the company with
the noble and obedient angels.

"For the one [me]
who recites with difficulty,
stumbling through its verses,
then he'll
have twice that reward."

When I tell Aaliyah that,
she says,
At least I save double or triple the time.

Still not fair.

What I Think About

At school,
I think about table tennis.
In Quran class,
I think about table tennis.

If I didn't have to do Quran class,
and I didn't have to go to school,
I'd probably be **even better** at table tennis.

But Amma says,
Quran class
and school
are *nonnegotiable*.

Seventh-Grade First Day of School

Ms. Morgan calls roll
says my name
like she's doing math:
Add-nan.

I tell her it's like
Ud-nahn.

In my mind
     if you can say *um*
     you can say *ud*;
     if you can say *nah*
     you can say *nahn*.
     Adnan.

But Ms. Morgan
doesn't try to say my name in her loud voice.
Instead, turns her lips into a line
just nods
and calls me Add-nan from then on.

(She didn't bother trying.)

Teacher Next Door

Ms. Potts once subbed for Ms. Morgan
and when I told her my name,
Adnan,
Like *ud* + *nahn*
her earrings nodded up and down.
She immediately tried to say it
and got it right on her second try.

It's not that hard!

Seventh-Grade Language Arts

Prose—
    Ms. Morgan
        says prose
           is made up of regular words all
           together.

But to me,
    prose
      is like
        pros
          and cons.

Pros—Summar is in this class.

Cons—Ms. Morgan is BORRRRRRRRRRRING.

Gum

Even Summar
doesn't love Ms. Morgan,
and Summar
loves *all* her teachers.

Even though
we aren't allowed to chew gum at school,
Summar will turn
when Ms. Morgan isn't looking,
hand me a skinny silver rectangle
with bright pink peeking through.
Then she'll turn back,
a swish of her bouncy black ponytail
while I nod thanks,
and we act like it never happened.

Ms. Morgan's Lesson

Poetry
is slicing
words up
and making them sing.
Maybe . . .
table tennis
is slicing
the ball down,
making my opponents lose.

Ms. Morgan's Voice

Her voice is too loud,
but when she gets mad it's too quiet.
She gives detention if you Y-A-W-N,
which is ridiculous.

What if you stayed up the night before,
watching table tennis strategies on YouTube
to get better and better

so that one day
you'll be ready for tournament playoffs.
And you're so excited
you don't get as much sleep?

Ms. Morgan's Challenge

Ms. Morgan is the
type of teacher
who thinks I should participate more,
smile more.

She click-clacked her way over to me
in heels that look like squares
said, *By the end of the year,*
I'll make you smile,
just wait and see.

Challenge accepted.

I decided right then
that I wasn't going to smile in her class.

Ms. Morgan goes about
learning who I am
the wrong way.
It's easy not to smile in her class.

Ms. Darlene is another story.

Ms. Darlene

My favorite adult in school
sprinkles powder on vomit,
sweeps up pencil shavings,
makes floors shine.

Even though some say
Ms. Darlene
is just a
janitor
or custodian,
to me,
she's everything.

Secret

Last year, at recess time,
I jumped down from the monkey bars
and ran over to Ms. Morgan,
who doesn't like being interrupted.
She had to finish her whole conversation
before I could ask
if I could use the restroom.

Ms. Morgan
nodded,
flicked a finger
to the restroom area,
kept talking to Ms. Potts.

The school building was quiet,
since almost everyone was outside,
I slunk to the restrooms
but I was late,
too late,
looked down
and thought of a story to spin.

Ms. Darlene
was refilling paper towels—
Wait a minute.

When she came back,
she handed
me a pair of clean pants.
Here.

Even though
my cheeks stung
with embarrassment,
my insides felt cool with
relief.

Ms. Darlene acted like it never happened.

Stories

When I spin a story for Ms. Morgan,
she listens.
When I spin a story for Ms. Darlene,
she listens, and
pauses
what she's doing,

rests her hands
on her mop handle,
so her heart can listen too.
I like when she interrupts my story
at the good parts with three words,

Is that so?
inviting me to say more.

Coach Khalil Gets It

I like that Coach Khalil doesn't say,
The game should be fun!
or *Remember, it's just a game!*
the way Abu does
if I lose.

Coach Khalil knows
that when we're smashing the ball
back and forth
the fastest I've ever done

and my feet are   p   p   i   g
   like kernels

my sweat d
                    r
                        i
                            p
                             p
                                i
                                  n
                                    g
                        like butter

that it's the most fun
I've had in a while,
that I'll keep coming back
for more.

Coach Khalil's Advice

Coach read something once
that he says
reminds him of me.
*"Great ones
are the ones
who absolutely hate losing.
They hate losing
more than*

they love winning.
That's what
makes them champions."

Coach Khalil points his paddle at me.
Losing is inevitable.
You can't avoid it . . .

When I frown,
Coach Khalil smiles
and the lines next to his eyes deepen
into a W.

If you lose, remember,
you need to be gracious.
Your opponent isn't your enemy—
it's all about sportsmanship.

But you can lose
a lot less . . .
and that's what I'm here to help with,
and you can bet that we're going to have fun doing it.

Coach Khalil leans over
holds his paddle up
and we high-five our paddles.

Tournaments

Coach Khalil
says table tennis is a beautiful sport,
a mix of strategy and skills
physics and art.

You have to be strong physically
but also mentally.

Coach Khalil
practices drill
after drill.
Says if I keep doing well,
then I can
start tournaments.

Finally!

So Far

I've only played my family,
and friends,
Summar (she has her own category),
Coach Khalil,
and a couple of kids at table tennis practice.

I've beat them all
(except Coach Khalil).

I've never played in a tournament before
but after a long volley with Coach Khalil,
I returned the ball
smooth and consistent each time
even when Coach Khalil hit the ball close to the net

lunge
and I had to hit it
or when he hit it on the corner of the table
and I had to stretch to hit it
I didn't miss a point
not one.

Coach Khalil pants,
wipes the sweat off his forehead,
says I'm ready to compete.

My feet

                    bounce

                                        spin

                                                  like the
                                                  table tennis
                                                  ball.

I see Abu get up from his chair
hug me even though I'm all sweaty
snap his fingers
yell,
Snap!
     Crackle!
               Pop!
I'm just about to tell Abu to stop
but Coach Khalil snaps too.

Table Tennis Tournament Stages

First are playoffs.
If you win,
you qualify and go on to the next,
the best of the best,
The Ultimate Table Tennis Championship
    Tournament.

I think I can do this.

More than anything . . .

I
        want
                to
                        win.

Calendar

A quick look.
The Ultimate Table Tennis Championship
    Tournament
takes place on Eid weekend.

My favorite cousin,
Idrees,
lives in Orchid, Florida.

I hop on to Google Maps.
My search shows promise.

The tournament takes place in Orlando.
Amma,
Orlando is just a couple of hours' drive from
Idrees, Ibrahim, Ismail, Danish, Muna Khala, and Moez
    Khalu.

Could we see the cousins?
For Eid weekend?
Could we rent a house,
like we sometimes do?

I spread my arms up high
and spell *VACATION* in aviation alphabet.
Victor **A**lfa **C**harlie **A**lfa **T**ango **I**ndia **O**scar **N**ovember
Rizwan holds his arms out in a GIANT V.
Aaliyah twirls
tries to pat my head on each twirl
but I dodge out of her way.
Aaliyah says,
I know sometimes I don't believe in you
but this time I need to believe in you
because I want to go on a cousin vacation.
Don't let me down!

Amma doesn't know the answer yet,
but her lips turn up slightly,
and her eyes trace the numbers on the calendar.
Her hand pats her tummy,
circles one, two, three.
We'll see, inshallah.

Then Amma's eyebrows stand up.
Don't you have to qualify first at the playoffs?
I shrug.
It'll be easy.
I smile at my siblings.

I'm
Charlie
Oscar
November
Foxtrot
India
Delta
Echo
November
Tango

I—

    we—

        may have a chance.

Drills

At table tennis practice today
after stretches,
Coach Khalil leads me to a table
with
a machine-robot-looking thing
that has one eye.
Drill time!

says Coach Khalil,
turning the machine on.

The machine whirrs
before it spits out balls
straight at me.

Easy!
I return the ball.

Coach Khalil
raises his eyebrows
chuckles, *Ready to pick up the pace?*
He turns a knob higher
presses another button.

The balls spit out much faster.
And this time they zoooooooom

                                        to the right

and to the left

                    and straight at me.

I return only a few balls.
I can't keep up
no matter how much I try.
Doubt

d

    r

       i

          p

            s

                in my mind

like the sweat d

        r

          i

           p

             p

                i

                g

                d

                o

                w

                n

              my face.

Slow it down!
I gasp.

Coach Khalil turns the knob down
slightly.

I will. Don't worry. In the meantime, let's speed up your
  reflexes!

Practice with Summar

After drills
and after Quran class

              p
I run   u   the hill
to play basketball with Sufian.

After basketball, Sufian and Summar
run   d

        o

            w

                n

the hill to my house to see Riz.

Summar spins Riz round and round
before handing him to Sufian,
who says, *My turn!*
Sufian sits with Riz
builds wooden trains round and round

the room, looping under the coffee table
all the way to the table tennis table.

Summar walks over to the table tennis table
that sits in the middle of the dining room
picks up the paddle
twirls it.
Want to play?

Even though Sufian plays table tennis,
he doesn't love it
doesn't play as well
as Summar.

Summar hits the ball back
smoothly
easily
makes me work.

Even though I beat Summar
I think if I didn't practice as much,
I'd be in trouble.

Eid on the Horizon

I practice with Coach Khalil;
I practice with the machine;
I practice with Summar;
I practice with Abu;
I practice to get quicker

                            stronger
                                    better.

I notice my stamina is better too.
I can play for longer
and I don't sweat as much.

I tell my cousin Idrees about my progress
how I'm getting more consistent
how I hope we get to see him for Eid.

Idrees and I share the same birthday
although he was supposed to be older.
I was due May 1.
He was due April 1.
I came two weeks early.
He came two weeks late.
He's still older

just by a few hours.
He was born at Fajr time,
before the sun woke up,
I was born at Maghrib time,
as the sun was going to sleep.

We rarely see each other
on our birthday
but when we're lucky we get to see each other
on Eid.

I want Eid to be epic.

Seeing my cousins is THE BEST.

Eid Rituals

Early-Morning Alarm
Scratchy Shalwar Kameez
New Bar of Soap
Hot Eid Shower
Loud Masjid Khutbah
Buzzing Crowds of Families
Masjid Goody Bags

Crisp Dollar Bills
Drive-Through Doughnuts
Wrapped-Up Presents
Sour Patch Watermelon Candy
Peaceful Napping Parents
Extra Video Game Time!
With cousins it'll be **double** the fun.

Days I Used to Practice

Monday
Wednesday
Friday

Days I Practice Before
the Ultimate Table Tennis
Championship Playoffs

Monday
Tuesday
Tuesday
Wednesday
Thursday
Friday
Saturday
Sunday

Tuesdays

Yes, I know that's two Tuesdays.
I get up before school and practice with Abu,

then with Coach Khalil after school,
turning Tuesday into
TWOSDAY.

New Gift

Abu knocks on my door
hands me a gift
a gift before Eid
a gift for just me.

Sitting here with Abu
makes me feel
like I'm all grown up,
not so small anymore.

A watch
that has a tiny analog clock,
as well as a digital clock,
an alarm,
a timer,
and a pedometer, or step counter.

The watch is a grown-up-person watch
not a watch for little kids
(like Riz).

To beat new records!
says Abu.

To beat new people!
I tease Abu.

To have FUN and, sure, beat some people too
while you're at it!
Abu chuckles.

Now let's get Riz away from that Bubble Wrap and
wrapping paper!
Abu grabs Riz,
who is shredding wrapping paper
stomping on Bubble Wrap
throws him up high
so Riz forgets about the paper,
explodes into laughter instead.

Steps I Take in a Day When I Play Table Tennis

I average around eleven thousand or twelve thousand!

But when I babysit Riz,
It's almost fifteen thousand.
Rizzie never stops moving!

I think he'll be a great athlete
like me!

Prepping for the Playoffs

New shoelaces
+
New haircut
+
New watch (from Abu)
+
Trusty old paddle
=
Success.

Colors

Coach Khalil knows I'm color-blind,
tells me that the International Table Tennis Federation
prefers blue tables over green ones,
because one in twelve males are color-blind.
Today I may get to play
on a different-colored table.
Cool!

My First Table Tennis Tournament Playoff Ever

Usually at practice I hear
just the tap tap of the ball
against my opponent,
an opponent I usually know.

Here in a **giant**-sized gym
under too-bright lights
I see the blue tables.
(Which for me could also be purple.)

I hear many taps,
shoes squeaking,
a few **yells**
some cheers
some claps.

The tournament air
feels electric.
It feels like
there are Coca-Cola bubbles
in my tummy.

Looking Around

I see the competitors' volleys

back and forth.

So quick!
     Maybe too quick?
Worries
     bounce
          in
               my
                    mind.

A Question I Don't Really Ask Myself . . .

What if I'm not good enough?

Audience

I look at Riz
Aliyah
Abu
Amma
Coach Khalil.

Coach Khalil gives me a thumbs-up.
Abu looks at me, snaps twice
smiles his medium smile.
Amma isn't looking
because she's grabbing Riz from climbing the bleachers
and I wish she was paying attention
to me.
Just me.

Normally Aaliyah's looking
at her phone.
This time she gives me a thumbs-up.
A look I read as
Don't mess up . . .
I want a Cousin Vacation Weekend!

Warm–Up Stretches

I swing my legs
side to side
shake them out

l
      e
  f   x   my fingers.
I know I can do this.
I say a quick prayer.

Bismillah.

Four-Letter Word I Don't Let Myself Say

L-O-S-E.

Game Time

The match starts off
full of promise
when I get to serve first.
But it quickly goes downhill
when my opponent,
a kid bigger than me,
with glasses that slip off his nose,
has a serve I've never seen before.
His serve is fancy
full of
      spin
           and
                bounce.
His spin makes my ball

                    bounce

                                too right,

    too left,

                missing the table,
                landing into failure.

Uh-Oh

I peek over at the bleachers.
Losing makes me feel
like a punch in the stomach.

Riz doesn't get it
calls my name
waves to me
over and over.

I see Abu's fingers folded tightly
not snapping like how he does
when I win a difficult point.

I can tell the way Abu rubs his head
back and forth,
he's worried too.

Another Try

He wins the first set.
After we pause to drink water,
wipe sweat,
I try again.
Aim the ball back just so,
manage to return more this time
onto the purply blue.

I think like Coach Khalil.
Strategize.
Concentrate.
I notice a pattern—
his backhand is weaker.
I know what to do this time.

The corner of the blue table
winks at me.
When it's my turn to serve,
I aim
directly toward his back hand.

Much better!

Update

The good:
I have one set.

The bad:
He has one set too.

THE LAST GAME THAT DECIDES EVERYTHING . . .

10–10.
Tiebreaker.
I need to win the next two
match points.

I change up the pace,
hitting the ball back
slow and smooth

Before smashing it   d

                o

                w

                n

                            fast.

Toss the ball up,
try to disguise the spin that I'm going to add,
add a little spin to my serve—

Once

Twice

I'm in.

Celebration Time

Coach Khalil
runs over
high-fives me
tells me I played just right
that I made a great comeback.

Abu snaps his fingers.
Cheers.
Snap!
Crackle!
Pop!

Riz hugs my knees.
Amma flattens my hair.
Aaliyah says,
Not bad!

PART 2

WEIGHT
The gravitational
force that pushes
down.

Cousin Vacation

Road trip from Atlanta, Georgia,
      to Orchid, Florida—
Even though there's
      too many crumbs,
      too much noise,
      too many miles,
there's never too much anticipation
for a cousin vacation!

When the cousins are finally together,
we laugh louder.
The moms relax more.
Their biscuits become mush in their tea.
They fan themselves with magazines,
while we swim in the pool.

The pool house
has a gumball machine,
a popcorn machine,
a cotton candy machine,
a snow cone machine.
and a table tennis table.
What does it not have?

Night Before

After two days of
Popsicles that dye your tongue purple,
sunrays that hug your skin brown,
pool water that shimmers and invites you closer,
I never want cousin vacation to end.

But now that the tournament is tomorrow
it feels like there are popcorn kernels
popping in my tummy.

I'm nervous.

The Next Morning

The kernels in my tummy
are still popping
and I'm not hungry.

Abu insists, *You've got to eat—*
otherwise, you'll have breakfast-itis.

I raise my eyebrows
start to protest
but he hands me a plate of
eggs all scrambled up.

I only take a few bites.

Sufian's eggs are way better
but I don't tell him that.

Aaliyah's Try

In the background
Aaliyah cracks eggs
Riz whisks batter in the bowl and on counters
Aaliyah rummages for a pan.

Here.

Aaliyah slides the plate of eggs away
puts a pancake down instead.
I added extra chocolate chips.

Aaliyah turns.
The *S* of her hair
turns too
and I realize
Aaliyah really cares
wants me to win too.

This time, the kernels stop popping.
Riz and I eat the whole pancake.

Ultimate Table Tennis Championship Tournament

Usually it's just Coach Khalil,
maybe my parents
and siblings.
But this time,
it's lots of heads watching,
too many.
My cousins Idrees, Danish, Ibrahim, Ismail,
Rizzie,
who still has a smudge of chocolate on his chin
from morning pancakes
and Aaliyah, who's sitting up

phone turned down in her palms
actually paying attention.

Why I Like Fractions

Quarterfinals
        won

Semifinals
        won

Finals . . .
        I better win!

Lunch Break

I'm feeling extra confident
as I slurp spicy noodles,
so many that even my cousin Idrees
gives me a look.

Idrees is one foot taller than me
but eats much less than I do.
I don't get it.

Idrees high-fives me before my game
points to the huge golden trophy
tells me I'm really close.

I study the guy I'm going to play next.
I'm competing in the under-fourteen-year-old bracket.
The next guy must be way younger than me.

My opponent
is tiny,
hits the ball calmly,
slow even.
I tell Idrees,
Piece of cake.

Finals

My words to Idrees
mock me.

This guy may not have the fanciest serve
or the best spin,
but he has one thing
that I failed to notice—
Consistency.
Stamina.
This guy
never misses the ball!

My New Plan

I pick up the pace,
hit the ball faster,
harder,
get sweatier.

Usually I'm the one
with the game face
that doesn't change,
that stays neutral,
until I win.

But this guy
doesn't miss the ball,
doesn't smile either,
just keeps on playing.

Doesn't matter what strokes I use.
Even though I add—
underspin.
Topspin.

He creams me.
He beats me.
Bad.

This guy was saving up all his smiles
till the very last point.
Because when he wins,
he yells,
laughs long,
pumps two fists to the ceiling.
He cheers real loud,
then shakes my sweaty hand.

Runner-Up

Making it to the finals
but not winning
makes my feet feel really heavy.
I don't look at my family—
all I want to do is
hide.

Not sure why it's called
runner-up,
when I feel so

d
o
w
n.

What Abu Doesn't Say

Snap!

  Crackle!

    Pop!

Which is fine with me
because I've snapped,
crackled,
and am pretty pooped.

What Abu Does Say

There's always next time!
Think of how far you've come . . .

Feeling Up Again

But when my name's called
and my family cheers—
four cousins,
two uncles and aunts,
two siblings,
two parents,
all ten cheering for me,
I look at them all smiling—
it doesn't feel so bad anymore.

Pool House Counter

A second-place silver medal
shines on the kitchen island,
gleams so bright.
When you look at the medal,
your reflection glows back at you.

This must be what almost-success feels like.

On the Way Home

After the tournament
when my sweat's all dried
and my legs feel tingly,
we stop at Dairy Queen
to get ice cream cones.
My fingers feel the best type of cold.

High Off Family

On squishy sand
under screaming gulls,
we let the waves tickle our toes.
Slurp ice cream,
nibble on cones,
celebrate how far I've come.
Mint chocolate chip ice cream
tastes like vacation.

Amma's Camera

Amma snaps photo after photo
of the family.
Rizwan has chocolate ice cream on his chin,
sand in his hair,
and fistfuls of shells.

An older couple
with lots of wrinkles
and smiles,
give Rizwan
a special shell
with speckled dots,
little ridges
that feel like
baby teeth.
Enjoy!

Riz jumps up and down
with his special shell.
Amma snaps a photo of him.
Black silhouette jumping in joy,
while the sky and sea
swallow up
the egg-yolk sun.

FaceTime

After we pray Maghrib
Amma lends me her phone
so I can FaceTime Sufian
let him know I came in second.
Instead of Sufian picking up,
Summar does.
This time, happy kernels in my tummy
pop like popcorn
because I get to talk to Summar,
because I get to tell her first.
When she asks how I did
and I show her my silver medal,
she gasps.
I tell her *Thanks for practicing with me!*
and she smiles so hard her nose scrunches.
I'm sure you'll win lots more!
Her face disappears
when Sufian grabs the phone from her.
I wish I could tell Summar more
all about the game
and how I really feel.

I tell Sufian I didn't win the gold
but still Sufian **whoops** when I show him the
   silver medal.
yells I KNEW IT!
texts right after
   WE'LL CELEBRATE WHEN YOU GET BACK!!! 😊🏆🏆
   DON'T HAVE TOO MUCH FUN WITHOUT ME!!!

followed by another text

   This is Summar using Sufian's phone
   Tournament Details? 😊

My fingers fly as I type.

Eid

Eid on your own is fun,
but Eid with cousins =
way better.

At home I smile a little,
but with the cousins
I smile **a lot**.

Day Before Eid

The moms are ironing the Eid kurtas
and making us try them on,
which is the worst,
especially when we are doing
cannonballs
into the pool.

Amma pulls Rizwan over
while he slings his toy jellyfish back into the pool.

Amma dries fat raindrops off
his skinny back,
removes his floaty puddle jumper,
lays it on the pool chair
and puts the new kurta on.

Perfect! she coos.
Rizwan stops crying,
and spins,
the fabric floating
around.

Okay, I need the kurta back to iron now.

Rizwan hugs the kurta
shakes his head,
yells *NOOOOOOOOO,*
lips stretched into a smile.

He gallops round and round,
and laughter bubbles
out of my mouth,
to see him with a kurta on top,
swimming trunks on the bottom.

You're a funny little one,
aren't you?

Amma rumples his wet hair.
Let's take a swimming break.
Want a snack?

Snack Time

All the boys
(and Aaliyah)
are out of the pool
in seconds.

Kitchen

The smell of a pot of kheer for Eid,
cardamom milky sweetness
hugs us
when we walk in.

Amma plunks Riz
on a too-big-chair
that swallows him up.

Okay, not a messy snack for Rizzie
says Amma, giving me a look
as I lick my fingers
and slather Nutella on bread.

I don't want him to mess up his new kurta—
I'm going to make sure the iron's off.
Be right back,
Amma hollers to us.
Keep an eye on Riz . . .

I reach into the pantry
drop a scoop of Goldfish crackers
into a bowl
in front of him.

Rizwan's eyes shine
but his mouth pouts,
I want my jawwyfish.

You like fish too much!

Riz ignores me
Counts Goldfish crackers
One . . . two . . . three . . . four . . . five . . . seven . . .
     eight . . . nine . . . ten . . . eleven-teen.

The kitchen is noisy.
We are seeing
who can eat the most Nutella.
Idrees knows it's going to be me
when Amma asks,
Where's Riz?

He was right here a minute ago . . .

But Amma isn't asking anymore.
She's waddling,
running
to the porch's open door
that leads downstairs to the pool.

We are right behind her.

Frozen

I see Rizwan in the water
the weight of it pushing him down,
arms stretched out
toward the jellyfish
on the pool floor . . .

My mind spins—
        But he's not dressed for swimming . . .
        But we already swam today . . .

Usually

The six of us are always talking,
but as we stare
and hold our breath,
we are silent.

This silence
is the worst thing
I've ever heard.

CPR

It must be bad,
because my uncle Moez Khalu is doing CPR.
CPR is what I learned in PE.
It is used to help someone
who is going to
die.

Is Rizwan going to . . .

Die?

Amma's voice
howling and hoarse,
praying loudly.

My prayers
urgent
a whisper
a plea.
Make him wake up!

CPR

Three letters.
You would think
something with only three letters wouldn't take
that many minutes.

While We Wait for Paramedics

My uncle
blows two breaths,
presses down,
over and over.
I don't realize my mouth is moving,
counting to thirty with him.
One . . . two . . . three . . . four . . . five . . . six . . .
seven . . . eight

Paramedics

It's not like the movies
with loud sirens everywhere.
Instead
a glaring flash of lights
and people in a big hurry.

        We step
back
      let them do their job . . .

Seconds

Feel like minutes,
as we wait for Rizwan
to wake up.

Wake up.
Wake up.
Wake up.

Ambulance

Amma's words to the paramedics—
I don't get it,
he was right there . . .
Will he be okay?

Amma, I think he wanted his jellyfish, I say in a small voice.
But no one hears me as the ambulance zooms away.

I wait for them
to turn on the siren,

I wait for them
to turn Riz back on . . .
Don't they know how to wake him up?

No one sees me scoop the jellyfish toy
out of the pool with the net.
I decide to
save it for Riz,
for when he gets back.

The Call

Amma and Abu are at the hospital,
while we stay back with Muna Khala and Moez Khalu
and wait what seems like many, many hours
And although we are with the cousins,
the easy laughter is sucked out of the room.

When the phone finally rings.
Muna Khala picks up.
And when she turns,
she doesn't look like Muna Khala,
doesn't sound like her anymore.

She wilts to the floor.

The moment
we realize that Riz
isn't coming back,
I take my table tennis medal
and slam it on the counter,
with all my weight.
When I look at my reflection
within it,
I'm cracked.

I Don't Get It

Moez Khalu is a doctor,
he knows CPR.
He reached Rizwan after what felt like just a minute,
we were all right there.

But it doesn't matter—

It was too late.

We were too late.

Retest

Back in school
when we didn't do well,
if we failed at something,
Ms. Morgan
gave us a retest.

But there is no retest now.

Time

The time it takes
for a toddler to drown—

thirty seconds.

Drowning

It's not like in the movies
where someone is loud.
It's quick.

Quiet.

And then,

you're

all

alone.

All Riz Wanted

All he wanted
was to get his jellyfish.

He thought the water was his friend.

He thought that he could swim.
He was wrong.
Very wrong.

Without his floats,
the water was his enemy.

Abu always says,
Watch out for your baby brother.
But I didn't watch him . . .
and now he's gone.

Aaliyah's Three Words

Aaliyah is usually loud
talks a lot
but right now
she isn't talking.
Instead, she sniffs
sobs
whispers

> *I'm so sad*

> *I'm so sad*

> *I'm so sad*

over and over.

My eyes aren't crying
but inside I am.
I whisper back
so only she can hear
Me too.
Me too.
Me too.

Survival

Muna Khala grabs her keys
says she's going to the hospital
to check on Amma and Abu,
but she doesn't say Riz.

When Aaliyah asks if she can tag along,
I ask too.

Under fluorescent lights,
Nurse Bella squeezes Amma's hands.
I'm praying for y'all.

Nurse Bella's
dark brown eyes glaze with tears.

Nurse Bella tells us
        that there are infant and toddler
        swim survival classes,
        that puddle jumper floaties
        give little children
        a false sense of security.

Abu's voice wavers,
c r a c k s.
You know when we leave the hospital
with a brand-new baby
it's all about the car seat . . .
making sure we can get home safely.
Why don't they talk about water safety,
how common it is, drowning?
Why don't they tell us
about water survival classes?

The Problem with Floats

They hold kids up
vertically.

We thought it was cute
when Riz would bicycle in the water,
but the problem is
the

v
e
r
t
i
c
a
l

position
is the drowning position.

Dr. Olliver's Sad Fact

Did you know
the leading cause
of accidental death
for kids aged one to four
in the United States
is drowning?
Riz was two years old.

The Ride Back to the Beach House

Amma and Abu
are still at the hospital
and I still don't believe
that Riz really isn't
coming back.

Sofa

Before,
Amma would sit on the floor
open her arms wide
like airplane wings
and Riz would run straight into them
like a runway
while Amma laughed and tickled him.

When Amma and Abu return from the hospital
without Riz,
they shuffle to the sofa,
their faces broken.

Amma and Abu
see me and Aaliyah
really see us.
Abu opens his arms wide,
then Amma.
Aaliyah and I walk into them
and instead of Amma laughing
Amma cries.

Idrees's Fort

Idrees watches us
with red eyes
slides the door open outside, and comes back in
covers my parents, Aaliyah, and me with a blanket
that smells of sunscreen and beach sand.

When we were little,
Idrees and I would use blankets to build forts
but with my parents and Aaliyah under the blanket
Idrees nods at me.
He knows this is the fort
I need.

A Word That Haunts My Mind

If

I hadn't qualified for the Ultimate Table Tennis
    Championship . . .

If

we hadn't come to Florida,

would Riz still be here?

I Wish

I wish
I never qualified
for the tournament.
I wish
I never played
table tennis.
I wish
we never came
to Florida.

If we hadn't come here,
my brother—
my baby brother
would still be alive.

PART 3

DRAG
Drag is the
force that resists
movement.

Janaza Prayer for Burial

I thought **big** boys
weren't supposed to cry,
but then
why are the men
crying?

I guess
when something is sad enough
boys and men
do
cry.

The Florida Masjid

The masjid is decorated
with Eid balloons,
streamers,
and candy.
Normally I'd be having fun,
racing around,

feeding Riz candy.
But I'm here for a funeral.

Riz's funeral.

Muslim Rules

When someone dies,
they are buried almost immediately.

Riz has been washed,
is mostly covered,
and even though we don't know
these people in the masjid here in Florida,
I wish they'd known Riz
how if he was here

      he'd take the men's car keys during prayer time
      he'd run through the masjid, not walk
      he'd laugh like happy fireworks.

Janaza

Not everyone gets to see Riz,
but Amma lets Aaliyah and me take a quick look.
Aaliyah's face drips
and she holds my hand
squeezes
while we look at Riz.

Riz looks so still
like he's asleep,
but he's not.
His hair's still curled out a little,
not a lot
like it usually is,
so he looks different,
smaller.

If I were to hold him close
the way I used to at bedtime,
his head on my shoulder

wouldn't feel the same —
the language of his eyelashes
silent.

Why

When someone dies,
why does their name
disappear . . .
fade?

When did he
turn from
my brother, Riz,
into just
"the body"?

My Steps

It feels as if
an unseen engine must be powering my feet,
because I walk to the muddy graveyard
like everything's fine.
It doesn't feel real yet.
In the back of my mind
I keep thinking,

Where's Riz?

Aaliyah's Steps

Abu's eyes are red and watery
and he puts on his sunglasses,
the ones he usually wears for vacation
even though this isn't a vacation anymore.

Aaliyah walks and stops
eyes leaking still.

I reach out
hold her hand.
Abu puts his hands on our shoulders
while Amma holds us tight.

Slowly, one step at a time,
we keep walking.

Rules of Life and Death

This is not supposed to happen to brothers,
(baby brothers especially).
It's supposed to happen to old people,
(really old people).

The Next Day

Even though
the sun is bright,
Even though
the sky is a cloudless blue,
Even though
the waves are calm,
we stay inside.

Amma and Abu
are broken.
So we sit and wait,
but we're waiting for someone
who isn't going to return.

Sunset

Our silence is broken
by my cousin Ismail—
I'm hungry.

Muna Khala wipes her eyes.
Amma shuffles to the fridge,
peers left to right,
but there's no milk
no eggs.

Today is the day
we were supposed to leave,
as a happy family.
But we're still here,
a sad family.

Amma hangs her head,
silently sobs,
There's no milk . . .
while Muna Khala hugs her,
patting circles on her back.

I know Amma's not crying over the milk.

Before Sunset

Usually
the grown-ups take a walk
while we play on the sand.
Now Aaliyah, Idrees, and I
smush our faces to the window,
because looking at the faces of the adults
is too hard.

It feels as if there's
a balloon pressing into my face,
pressing
behind my eyes,
my nose.

Pressing.
Pressing.
Pressing.

Doorbell

Before sunset
the older couple
with lots of wrinkles
and lots of smiles,
usually go on their walk.

But now
they come by
without shells,
without smiles.

Their wrinkles point down.

We heard.
We saw the ambulance.
We're so sorry.

Amma tries to nod
but instead cries harder.
The lady brings her close.
Now now.
Now now.

And those two words
bring Amma ease,
make her quiet.

The Old Lady

Older than Dadi and Nani,
the old lady hears Ismail whine
about being hungry.

Idrees whispers to Ismail
to be quiet
hands him a granola bar
that Ismail swats away.

I'm hungry too,
but since Riz is gone,
it feels like my stomach has been punched
inside out.

She doesn't ask if we've eaten.
Instead, she whips out her phone,
What toppings do you like on your pizza?

Thirty Minutes until Pizza

We were going for our walk.
We missed seeing you—
come.

Maybe because he's really old,
maybe because he doesn't ask,
all of us listen
to the old man
whose voice is
like pebbles on the shore.

Riz's Ocean

Outside,
birds swim in the sky,
sunlight attacks my face.
But even though it's the same sun,
the same ocean,
everything feels different.

My aunt
Muna Khala
sniffles,
dips her hand
into frothy waves.
There's a hadith I heard—
"This life is like a drop of an ocean
and the next life is an ocean."

We'll get Riz in the next life,
she says, p a u s e s,
wipes a tear in the setting sun,
for an ocean.

Balloon

The balloon that fills my face
releases pressure,
pops.
Water falls from my eyes.

Night

A couple of knocks on the door,
on the porch steps we find
     a gallon of milk
     bread
     eggs
     cookies
     a note
        in loopy cursive,
Eat if you can.
Praying for you.
—Becky & Aaron

Amma's eyes rain tears again.

Road Trip Home

I put Riz's special shell
in my pocket,
a piece of Riz
for the road trip home.

At the Dunkin' drive-through—
Can I take your order?
Amma's voice is automatic.

One plain glaze
        for me,
One chocolate frosted
        for Aaliyah,
One strawberry icing with sprinkles
        for Riz.

She doesn't realize
until she turns around,
that we don't need
the car seat anymore.

We don't need
the doughnut.

Who knew
a crumply Dunkin' bag
with a strawberry icing with sprinkles doughnut,
could be so sad?

Sadness

An empty car seat
with no crumbs.

Our Family

Zakir party of five
left for Florida.
Now, we are returning as
Zakir party of four.

Did You Know?

News spreads fast.
Especially when it's
bad news.

In Our House

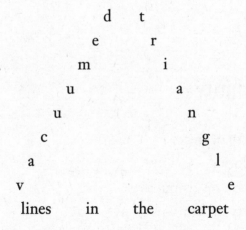

```
              d    t
            e        r
          m            i
        u                a
        u                  n
        c                    g
      a                        l
      v                          e
    lines    in    the    carpet
```

A vase of sunflowers (Amma's favorite)
A foiled dish of biryani with lots of sugary aloos (Abu's
    favorite)

A note from Mariam Aunty and Zohair Uncle (Sufian
    and Summar's parents)

A card to Aaliyah and me
with a big red heart drawn
a Band-Aid stuck in the middle
from Summar.

A note from Sufian
tightly folded
with just two words:
This Sucks.

And right now
I feel a teeny
tiny bit
better.

Three Days After

Amma's cried
so much,
her face looks like
puffy dough.
She has
slits for eyes,
her nose is pink,
her voice a shadow.

I wish it were me,
she says.
Abu pats circles into her back.

Amma Says

My dadi
used to
pray
for her children to
live

longer
than her.

To never
see her children die . . .

I wish I'd said that prayer more.

When Home Is Too Quiet

Time drags real slow.

Aaliyah's room:
the music is off.

Riz's room:
the door is closed.

My room:
I feel like I don't belong.

When Home Is Too Loud

Instead of greeting guests
who are here to give condolences,
I sit on my bed,
press the timer
on my new watch.
Thirty seconds—
the time it takes for a toddler to drown.
I press it over and over
until my face is wet.

Aaliyah's Route

I heard
pigeons have a good sense of direction
and know exactly where to fly,
because they can read magnetic fields.

Aaliyah is like that pigeon.
She knows
exactly where to find me.

Aliyah's room and mine
are separated by a bathroom,
and opposite our rooms
is Riz's.

Aaliyah sits by me,
as we both look across the hall.
We're not big huggers
but still,
she puts her arm on my shoulder.

Before Aaliyah would tease me
when I would cry if I lost a game,
calling me a spoilsport.
But she doesn't tease me for my tears.
She joins right in.

Before, when it was quiet,
Aaliyah would fill up the spaces
by talking and laughing.
But this time it's quiet
and it's okay.

Aaliyah's Question

Abu sees me and Aaliyah
sitting side by side
staring at Riz's room
hears Aaliyah whisper,
Do you feel like it's our fault—
Aaliyah gulps—
that Riz isn't here?

I nod
open my mouth
to say
All the time
but
Abu interrupts
kneels down
puts his hands on our shoulders
looks us in the eyes.

It's not your fault.
Not your fault.
Understood?

Aaliyah nods and sniffles
looks at me.

Abu sighs.
When did you last eat popcorn?

When we shrug,
he says, *I'll be right back.*

Abu's Delivery

In a few minutes
Abu hands over a bowl of
popcorn, the extra-buttery kind.

I know you said
if you went a day without popcorn
it felt weird
so here you go.

My buttery lips
whisper thanks.

Amma joins us too
eases herself and her big tummy to the floor
even though sitting on the floor
looks uncomfortable.
Amma sits on one end of us

Abu on the other
while all four of us
look into Riz's room.
Abu's arms hug.
Amma's hands pat our heads.

Coconut Oil

Amma's hands stop patting.
Adnan, can you get the coconut oil?
I grab the slippery jar
of smeary white goo
that sits on Amma's bathroom sink.

Just because my hair looks messy
(Amma's hair leaks from her bun)
doesn't mean yours has to be,
says Amma, who begins to braid Aaliyah's hair.
Amma unknots tangles
rubs oil into Aaliyah's head
until her fingertips shine.

What about me? jokes Abu.

Amma drops a drop making the top of his bald head
    shinier

then flicks a drop on my hair too.

I flinch.
Gross!

Amma smiles.
Now that you have some oil I might as well rub it in,
and because she looks like she's in a better mood
I let her rub it in
and
actually it doesn't feel that bad
actually maybe even a little good.

Now if only your hair would stay flat,
Amma says.

Maybe add some spit? Abu pretends to gargle.

GROSS! yell Aaliyah and I at the same time.

Amma Wonders

I wonder what type of hair the new baby will have,
Amma wonders.

Curls like Riz?
Waves like Aaliyah?
Straight hair like Adnan?

Or maybe no hair like me? chimes Abu.

Amma smiles.

Talking about a future
with a new person
feels a little
like light
again.

My Parents Words

Abu whispers to Amma
Amma stops brushing
stops braiding
cups Aaliyah's chin and mine
says, *What happened to Riz is not your fault.*

Amma looks into Aaliyah's eyes—
relief seeps into them.

Amma looks into my eyes next
waits for me to answer.
I nod
but
relief is something
I don't feel.

I know this has been hard. So hard.
You guys are doing a good job.
I want you to remember
what happened to Riz
it's not your fault.

I make my head nod again
lock my parents' words inside my heart
peek at Aaliyah's believing eyes,
but unlike Aaliyah I don't believe them.

                       won't believe them.

If I hadn't gone to Florida to play table tennis,

Riz would still be here.

The Days After

Our house
is full of people,
but even in this house
with so many people,
it would only take one person
for the house to feel full.

It Gets Harder

I overhear Nani Ami
tell the guests
about when Nana Abu died.
It's a lie
when they say
it gets easier with time.
Nani Ami shakes her head.

Her braid sways violently.
It gets harder . . .

The words repeat
in my head.

It gets harder . . .

At the Door

Coach Khalil has come.
I heard the news.
I'm so sorry.

You tell me
if you need a break.

A silence too long.
I turn to look at my table tennis table.
What used to bring me joy,

now brings me something else,
that feels like
dread.

I do.
I need a break.

If I hadn't qualified for the Ultimate Table Tennis
    Championship Tournament,

hadn't gone to the pool house,

would Riz still be here?

Reflection

Sometimes you don't see the ball coming,
it spins right by you.
Sometimes you don't see bad stuff coming either,
it spins right by you too.

Guests Come Every Single Day

Abba and I refill ice from the freezer.
Clang! Bang!
Something about the sound
reassures me.
If I'm moving, I'm not still.
If I'm still, I'm thinking,
thinking too hard
about Rizwan,
which makes my stomach turn.

The house smells too strongly of aunty perfumes,
which turn my sniffles into sneezes.
The house has too many scratchy kurtas,
which claw at my face

when aunties pull me in for hugs.

Why do they have to visit? I say,
over ice clanging.

We're a community. It's what we do.

There are six rights of one Muslim to another.
One of them is if someone dies, attend their funeral.
They couldn't attend in Florida, so they're here now.

What We Hear a Lot

Innalilahi wa innailahi rajioon
Verily to God
do we belong,
And to God
do we return.

Dadi wipes away tears.
Riz wasn't ours.
Never was ours.
He belongs to God—
we all do.

What We Also Hear

I'm sorry for your loss,
like we lost something small
a pen,
a ball,
a piece of luggage.

But we lost something HUGE.
A whole person.
My brother.
Rizwan.

Things I'm Tired of Hearing

I'm so sorry.
You're so brave.
You're so strong.
It's God's will.
It was written.
I can't imagine.

Well, here's the thing—
Why would you want to imagine?

(I wouldn't recommend it.)

Past Tense

Rizwan is

is now

Rizwan was

But it's hard to remember that
sometimes.

Everything Aches

Constipation

> When you don't eat right,
> sometimes the poop can't come out.

Grief

> When you don't feel right,
> sometimes the tears can't come out.

Cookies

Before,
when I peeled open
the top of the Chips Ahoy!,
the chewy chocolate chip kind
(Riz's favorite),
I'd automatically grab four cookies,
two for me,
two for Riz.
And I'd pour us two cups of milk.

Now

I'm stuck holding four cookies,
and I'm not hungry anymore.

Before,
cookies wouldn't stand a chance.
Now
nothing tastes or feels the same.

The Table Tennis Table

Before,
I would walk past the table
and my fingers would skim the surface,
twirl my paddle,
flick the ball,
and my worries away.

I'd challenge Abu,
practice a few serves.

Now
when I see the table
I don't go near it.

Instead,
I drag my feet
f   a   r   away.

Dadi

Dadi hugs me close,

pats the bones in my back,
says, *All I feel is haddi,*
cups my chin.

In the kitchen
it's just Dadi and me.

You need to eat.

But I'm not hungry.

Nonsense!
Dadi walks past
the counters of foil trays
(all the food from the aunties),
walks into the pantry,
grabs a crackling packet
of ramen noodles,
microwaves it,
and sprinkles masala.

Here.

But I'm not hungry
is on the tip of my tongue.

Eat.

Dadi gives me a look.
She knows I usually eat and eat
and have to be told to slow down.

This time
when I pass the trays of food,
rice buttered in ghee,
meat drenched in nihari curry,
and parathas flaky the way I like them,
I feel nothing.

The food doesn't invite me closer
the way it used to.

Eat

Dadi looks at me,
and I want to explain
but I don't know how.

She says,
This food is easier.
Eat.

Noodles
stained golden with turmeric,
saturated in spice,
glide down
easily.

This time
my stomach stops twisting,
and lets me keep the food down.

Condolences

Condolences are what people
are supposed to give,
but it feels like
all they do
is take.
Amma's tears.
Nani Ami's food.

Irony

You would think with
all the food in the house,
we would be eating
and **f u l l**.
But we're not.

Amma's face is thin,
even though her stomach isn't.
Nani Ami sits her down,
force-feeds her by hand.

You've got to keep up your strength
for this new baby.
You've got to keep up your strength
to honor Rizzie.
Rizzie would want you
to keep on going,
to keep being a good amma.
Theek hai?

One Good Thing

Summar is in my house more.
But there are lots of people crying,
like Maya, another neighbor.

Maya's crying,
but she didn't even know Rizwan,
not the way I did.
Summar and I exchange a look,
a short one,
then a long one,
as if she's saying,
I get it.

Sufian's Route

Sufian rings the bell
every morning
in his checkered pajamas
drops off a paper plate of eggs
wrapped in crackling foil.

Sufian who isn't a morning person
doesn't say anything
just hands the plate over.

Sufian knows I like his eggs,
not other people's,
and doesn't hover to make sure I eat it,
just walks away
and I know he'll go back to sleep.

(Most days I eat it.)

Amma to Abu

A widow
is the word for when
a wife loses a husband.

Why is there
no word
for
when
a mom loses
her child?
Her baby?

Amma Moans

I hate being told
You're so strong,
so brave.

Give me a break.

It's Nothing Really

A small vibration,
a ding on Amma's cell,
an automated text.

Reminder!
Rizwan Zakir
is due for his
two-and-a-half-year appointment.

I think the pediatrician's office
needs to update their system.

Another Ignored Text

Carter's Thirteenth Birthday Bash
Pool Party
I'm not ready.

Laundry

Every time I do the laundry
I miss Riz.
Before, I'd pour a cup of blue detergent
and scent-boosting beads,
hand it to Riz to pour in.

Now I pour the detergent in,
Just me.

Amma bought new detergent
and it's unscented
because of her allergies, and
Abu hasn't bought
fragrance-booster beads in a while.

Laundry smells
feels like
nothing.

What We Have Too Much of

Smelly flowers.

What We Don't Have Enough of

Two-and-a-half-year-old brothers.

Flowers

Amma usually likes them,
especially the sunflowers
that move their heads to the sun,
but since Riz
the flowers lie on the counter,
shriveling up.

Aaliyah rips off the wrapper,
gets a vase,

fills it up
with water.

In My Room

Aaliyah finds me again.
This time she brings
Kit Kats.
She breaks the sticks—
two each.
Before we would break them
for the three of us,
and share the last bar
in crooked thirds.
One day we planned to
share them in perfect fourths,
each one of us
getting one stick each,
like Amma said.

As Aaliyah and I munch
on Kit Kats,
I wonder if she's thinking
the same thing.

She nudges me with her shoulder,
looks at Riz's room.
Do you ever imagine?

She leaves the silence hanging—
I know she's asking,
Do you ever imagine
that Riz is still here?

I nod.
All the time . . .
Sometimes when I wake up
for a second
I forget he's gone.
When I remember,
it's the worst.

Aaliyah nods.
Me too.
Two words that make me feel
less alone.

Coach Khalil's Route

Some guests avoid looking at me,
avoid talking to me,
but Coach Khalil rings the bell
invites me for a walk.

Coach Khalil
looks me in the eye.

I may know what you're going through.
I've been there.

My baby brother
died in a freak accident
on the playground.

It was the
weirdest thing—
the bluest skies,
a beautiful day.

I was on the swings,

he was going down the slide.
The cord on his hood
got caught . . .
The words
that have been stuck inside me,
waiting waiting waiting
scratch my throat —
I should have been watching him.
It's my fault.

Coach Khalil nods.
I should have been on the slide with him.

I didn't see it happen.
I wasn't fast enough.

I'm here
anytime you need to talk.

Don't go through it alone.
I'm here.

Grief

Is a language
I wish
I never had to learn.

Worst Condolence
Gift Ever

A sad aunty
gives us a sad plant,
with leaves that

D
R
O
O
P.

Sad Aunty talks and talks
pats Amma on the tummy.

Don't worry,
at least you have another
on the way.

Amma's face wilts
and all I want
is for Sad Aunty to leave
now.

I grab the vacuum
plug it in
start vacuuming
angry triangle lines into the carpet.

Aaliyah knows what I'm doing
swallows a smile
grabs a bottle of cleaning spray
        sprays
                    wipes
                            sprays.

With all the noise,
Sad Aunty stops talking
shuffles herself slowly to the door.

When Sad Aunty leaves,
I take the sad plant
and stuff it in the trash.

You Know What's Really Sad?

Sad Aunty didn't even know Riz.

Condolences

When Sad Aunty leaves,
Abu puts his head
in his hands.

Enough!
Let's do one meeting at the masjid.
Get this over with.
No more guests!

Saved by the Bell

Sufian rings the bell,
asks if I want to play ball.

I wasn't sure
if you needed more time,
but my mom sent me over . . .

I look over my shoulder
into the sadness,
put the vacuum away,
lace up my shoes.
Let's get outta here.

Sufian's House

On top of the hill,
surrounded by trees that stretch for the sky,
is Sufian's house
and a basketball net.

Where's Summar?

Collecting bugs.
Sufian rolls his eyes.
What's up?

I tell Sufian,
Without Riz, even doing the laundry feels different.

Sufian listens
thumps as he bounces.
You know what?

What?

I once broke the washing machine. True story!
says Sufian.

I was collecting rocks,
left the rocks in my pockets.
My mom did the laundry,
didn't know the rocks were still in my pockets.
I got in BIG trouble!

Sufian chuckles
bounces the ball
into thump thump thump
swooshes the ball into the net
over and over.

Whenever Sufian scores,
he shimmies
making my lips curl up in the corners.

HEY! Sufian passes me the ball.
You're smiling!

Sufian shimmies again.
I smile once more.

When I'm Home

Abu laces up his shoes

asks, *Want to run?*

I shake my head.

asks, *Want to walk?*

I shake my head again.

How about a quick game of table tennis?

Abu holds the paddle out to me.

I shake my head harder.

In my mind,

> *Definitely not.*

Abu studies my face
looks at me like I'm a puzzle piece
he's trying to sort out.

Next time, inshallah.

Masjid Meeting

Abu set up a meeting today at the masjid
so we can meet everyone in one go
stop having guests.

Today the masjid doesn't smell like cinnamon
or melted sugar
or anything special
which means Sufian didn't bake or bring in anything

because he probably didn't feel like it
probably because there's no Riz to eat it.

Instead, all I see on a long white table
are a box of store-bought crummy oatmeal pies
and I hate that Little Debbie is smiling on the box.
I hate that oatmeal is a "dessert"
But most of all
I hate that Riz isn't here.

Little Shadow

Today at the masjid
Imam Talha
doesn't call me Big Shadow
doesn't call Riz Little Shadow.
Because Riz isn't here.

Aren't shadows supposed to be always there?

Masjid

The men's area is in the front
and the women's area in the back,
but Aaliyah and I sit
side by side
shoulder to shoulder
on the carpet.

I can feel the stares
that make my back hot
poke my back
when Riz is mentioned.

Today Imam Talha's voice
doesn't **boom**.
Instead his voice is
a scratch.
Imam Talha says,
On the Day of Judgment
in heaven,
we will be united with
those we lost.

Like in an airport,

*the departure lounge
is full of sad faces,
people saying goodbye.*

*The arrival lounge
is full of happy faces,
people meeting their loved ones.*

*Right now
it feels like there is no hope,
but remember
that we will definitely reunite.
Inshallah.
There is hope
for the believers.*

Airport Memories

Aaliyah pokes me.
Remember how we're always late for the airport?

I remember the last time we traveled
all five of us
Amma told me to run ahead to the gate

tell the gate agents we were coming.
As I ran
Riz cheered,
Run run run!

Remembering that makes me smile
but my smile dissolves
when I see a man looking at us
frowning.

He probably thinks we're fine
but if you were to look inside of me
inside of Aaliyah
we're still so sad.

A Prayer

Imam Talha prays for us—
Sabrun jameela
Beautiful patience.

Abu thanks everyone for coming,
starts to put the microphone back.
Amma waddles up.

Amma doesn't have a speech prepared,
but she grabs the microphone anyway.

Aaliyah and I exchange a look.
Worry
What's going on?

I don't want Amma
to cry into the microphone.
I don't want people to keep doing *the stare.*
They look at us,
then quickly look away.

My back feels hotter.

Amma's Speech

Even though Amma's tummy is full,
her face is empty.

What we're going through
is a parent's worst nightmare.
I don't want anyone
to ever go through this.

Water floats can give our children
a false sense of security,
that the water is all fun and games.

Please teach your little ones,
your babies,
to swim.
Her voice cracks.
To survive.

When I Overhear the Aunties

What a tragic accident . . .

But an accident
is when

you wet your pants,
spill your Cinnamon Toast Crunch,
fall off your skateboard,
miss the winning shot in table tennis.

An accident
is not when

someone drowns,
never to return again.

In the Masjid Lobby

I overhear people say,
Poor Aaliyah.
Poor Adnan.
I want to turn
and yell,
DON'T CALL ME POOR.

In the Boys' Restroom

In the stall,
I hear the voice of a boy.

My mom says,
it could have been prevented
if they'd watched him better.

I unlatch the door
step out into anger.

The boy sees my face,
shrugs into a sorry.

Sor—
Too late.

Lately
I've felt
sad
but now I feel
mad

even though I'm not
that **tall**,
I knock him over,
watch him squirm.
Don't you ever talk about my brother like that.
Got it?
The boy's eyes widen,
his mouth gapes,
he nods.
I need to hear you.
Or do you need me to drag you out
of here?
Got it. I'm really sorry.

I walk right out.

Sufian

My best friend sees my face
when I go back to the masjid prayer hall,
raises his eyebrows
but doesn't ask questions,
only asks
if I want to play basketball.
He doesn't ask
if I want to play table tennis,
because he knows I'm not interested
in that anymore.

I look over my shoulder
into the huddle of the aunties,
into the sadness.
I lace up my shoes again.
Let's get outta here.

PART 4

LIFT
Lift is the force that pushes an airplane up in the air.

Summar's Suggestion

I don't tell Sufian,
but when Summar also tags along,
I can't help but feel lighter.

With Sufian,
we play basketball.

When Sufian misses the hoop,
he runs down the driveway to get the ball.
and Summar turns to me.

What helped me
when Nani died,
was writing letters.
Summar's voice gets quiet.
I wrote to her.

But Riz can't read, I say.
Summar looks up,
does her slow blink,
scans the sky.

Sometimes when Summar speaks,
her sentences sound like questions.
But this time her voice is sure.

Maybe he can now . . .

At Home

Before, Amma cared about our screen time.
Now she doesn't.
Too much screen time.
Too many cousins.
But brothers—
not enough.

In My Mailbox

A sealed notebook
with a picture of a shiny beetle on the cover
a capped pen.

A note rolled up
thinner than a pencil
    Adnan,
    Use this
    to write letters
    to Rizzie.

I know who it's from.

Social Media

Aaliyah sits by the window
scrolls and scrolls
but when Taylor Swift's song blasts
"Never Grow Up"
Aaliyah throws her phone onto her bed.

That's a stupid song!
Want to play table tennis?

I don't like

how everyone asks me if I want to play table tennis

when the answer

is obviously

NO.

I shrug.
Not really.

I make an excuse:
we have Quran class soon.

Quran Class

Before Quran class,
Aaliyah hands me her Quran
the pages different colors of the rainbow
and all faded.
Can you test me?

I listen to Aaliyah
test her on her lesson
then revision

and even though Aaliyah still memorizes
quicker than me
barely makes a mistake,
this time I feel glad for her.

Aaliyah offers
to test me
and when I make mistakes
she doesn't make fun of me
or ask why I still don't know it
just sits down with me
has me read the ayah five times out loud
then repeat after her
over and over
until I finally get it.

Success!

When Aaliyah offers me her hand
for a high five,
I high-five right back.

In My Pocket

I put a piece of Riz
in my pocket—
his special shell
with the baby teeth ridges,
and speckles of brown.
The shell that was given to him
on the squishy sand.

My fingers
touch the shell
when I think about
my first day back at school.

My fingers
touch the shell
when I think about
how Riz won't drop me off,
how people will look at me
with pity.

My fingers
squeeze the shell hard.

First Day Back at School

Ms. Morgan says all the wrong things.
I'm sorry for your loss.
He sounded like he was
a great little brother.

Was.
Was.
Was.

What about *is*?

The Right Words

Ms. Darlene takes off bright yellow gloves,
washes her dark brown hands,
puts them on my shoulders.
Says I'm the reason she comes to work.

When she says that,
I believe it.

It reminds me of when
Amma and Abu would pray
for us kids
to be the coolness
of their eyes.

So whenever Amma or Abu would look at us
they would feel at peace
refreshed.

A prayer that made us—
me—
feel special.

Sanitation Engineer

I open my mouth to say, *Thank You,*
but it doesn't come.
Instead, I say,
Do you need help?

Ms. Darlene looks at me
and I think she's going to do the

I feel sorry for you face,
but instead she nods,

tosses me a clean pair of gloves.
Sure.

My hands
like squeezing the sponge,
like the release of bubbles,
like the shine of the counter,
like making something better.

Now

Instead of hurrying home
like I used to,
I linger after school,
where time drags less.
I don't like going home,
being reminded,
of who isn't there.

Summar's Gift

When Summar tags along with Sufian to my house,
she no longer brings toy cars or planes with her,
or smiles,
or magic tricks.

But today in class
she reaches into her pocket,
a swish of black bouncy ponytail,
hands me not one skinny silver rectangle but two.
And I hold the gum
that's still warm,
and let it warm me too.

Sufian's Gift

A ring of the bell
A **pound** on the door
Sufian on the porch
holding something out to me
that's not a basketball
or a plate of eggs.

Sufian doesn't give me gifts
but he hands me a Kroger plastic bag.
In it sloshes a brand-new blue bottle of All detergent.
It's scented Fresh Rain
but smells much better
so you can get a break from that unscented stuff.

Sufian swirls it
unscrews the cap
sticks it under my nose to smell.

I came to help you do laundry.

Sufian doesn't wait for my answer
takes off his shoes
clomps inside.
Tosses his shoes by the door
walks with me to the washing machine.

I dump in my clothes
drizzle in the detergent
pause
inhale the scent in
exhale out.
Sufian says,
Did I ever tell you the time I broke the washing machine?
Even when I nod
Sufian chatters the whole time

tells me the story again
distracts me,
which is what I need.
Laundry feels like something again.

Aquarium Field Trip

Before, Amma would sometimes chaperone
my field trips,
but she's due any day.
So she sends
    Abu in her place,
    along with peanut butter and jelly sandwiches
    sliced in diagonals,
    even though that's how Rizzie liked it (not me).

In the dark room
there are too many people,
huddled by glass.

When I walk closer,
I see it.
Lights shine right on the
jellyfish,

a golden yellow
in front of bright blue.

Tentacles—
red
orange
yellow
waving
fluttering
at me.

The jellyfish
reminds me of Rizwan,
the way he must have grabbed for his jellyfish toy
the way the water must have sucked him up.
It feels like
there is something sharp
in my throat
something pointy
pinching my nose.

And I feel so sad
that I don't even notice
the tears that slip
out of my eyes.

Abu

Abu puts his arm around me,
his forehead to mine.
          It's okay, Dani,
          It's okay.
And the way his voice cracks
tells me it's not okay,
which makes me feel like
we're both in it
together.

It's not okay.

          You're right. It's not okay.

I was right next to him when he disappeared.

          Dani, I was taking a nap,
          Abu chokes a sob.
          I was sleeping when he drowned.

I hold Abu.
Abu holds me.

All you can hear
is the two of us
heaving tears.

Abu breaks the silence.
> *It's not okay,*
> *but it will be.*
> *It will be.*
> *Inshallah.*
> *One day.*

Abu's Words

This time when Abu speaks to me
tells me it's not my fault
I don't need to fake nod.
I believe them.
In my eyes,
relief seeps.

1:07 a.m.

When Amma's water breaks,
Amma wakes Abu,
Abu wakes Aaliyah,
Aaliyah wakes me,
I wake no one.

When Abu rushes Amma to the hospital,
Aaliyah and I try to go back to sleep.
But now I know that sometimes
hospitals become places
where people die.

So instead of feeling excited
about Amma going in,
dread keeps me awake.
Until I hear the good news.

Hope

Is a feeling
I could get used to.

New Baby

Under the bright lights
in the hospital,
seeing Amma
holding a baby,
makes me feel sad
but happy too.

I missed seeing her
hold someone so
small.

Nusaybah

The baby
is named after a warrior in Islam.
We need a strong name
to live up to Rizwan,
says Abu.
This one's our warrior princess.

Nusaybah's Looks

Apricot-colored cheeks
popcorn-sized hands
gray eyes
deep and big
like upside-down sky.

Her hair smells
like the brown sugar
Abu sprinkles on his Rice Krispies.

When I hold her,
her weight feels
Just right,
like a perfect football.
(Except much cuter.)

How My Family Calms Nusaybah

When the sun gets ready to set,
Almost time to pray maghrib

Nusaybah **wails**.

Abu yells, *Family relay time!*
grabs Nusaybah,
runs a lap,
then passes her to Amma, who runs a lap
then Aaliyah
then me.

And whenever we run laps with Nusaybah
from one side of the kitchen
to the other side of the family room,
she stops crying.

How I Calm Nusaybah

When Nusaybah cries,
I swaddle her tight
the way Abu showed me how,
the way I used to for Riz.

When she still cries,
I cradle her head underneath my chin
and tuck her in.

Lean one foot forward
    rock forward
then back
    again
and again
until her cries turn into snuffles.

I memorize the language of her eyelashes
as she falls asleep.

How Aaliyah Calms Nusaybah

Nusaybah cries and cries
Aaliyah yells, *I've got this!*
grabs her Hula-Hoop,
the one with the rattling beads in it,
lays Nusaybah down on her mat
swirls the hoop around her
round and round
without stopping.

Nusaybah's gray eyes open wider
and don't blink
but then she closes her eyes
opens them again
closes them again.

Nusaybah lets the
whoosh whoosh sound
lull her
to sleep.

Pretty cool trick if you ask me!

When the Sunlight Is Bold

Aaliyah holds Nusaybah close,
puts on music and bounces,
swishes around the room.

When the nighttime is **bolder**,
Aaliyah puts on the Quran
plays the verses of Surah Mulk,
recites and sways Nusaybah softly to sleep.

Postpartum

It's the word for the six weeks
it takes for moms to heal
right after having a baby,
but Amma still isn't healed
after losing one.

Sometimes Amma
sighs <small>small.</small>

Sometimes Amma
sighs big.

Sometimes she's a little happy
and a lot sad.

Sometimes she's a lot sad
and a little happy.

The moods of Amma
come like waves,
like the ocean.
      Sometimes choppy
      sometimes gentle
      sometimes rough
anything but stagnant.

From the Window

I see Amma
parked
in the driveway,
pounding the steering wheel
over and over,

before laying her face on it
like it's a pillow
and crying.

Today is choppy.

Abu's Solution

Abu mixes
three cups of water
a half cup of white vinegar
grabs a soft cloth.

Abu d
    i
    p
    s
the soft cloth into the solution
wipes the legs
then the surface
of the table tennis table
until the dust is gone
and the table shines.

Looks good, doesn't it?

When I nod,
run my hands on the smooth surface,
Abu asks,
Want to play?

When Abu's not looking,
I pick up my paddle.
The weight feels all wrong,
and I quickly put it back down.

I shake my head.
My answer a surprise.
Not yet.

The *yet* arches in my mind
like a rainbow after a storm.

Before

If there was a stray ball,
Riz would scramble
crawl under the table,
smile and hold it up
like a precious gem.
He'd laugh so hard
his tummy wobbled.
He'd run round the table,
and I'd tickle him so hard
he'd drop the ball
and run away.

I don't miss the tap tap of the ball.
I miss the rhythm of his laugh.
I miss him building train tracks under the table.
I wish he were still here..

Things I Love about Nusaybah

Whenever she sneezes, she makes a tiny sound after,
a little baby coo.

The spiky *l*'s of her hair.

Whenever you take her out of her car seat,
she looks like she's stretching so far
but she's so tiny,
which isn't very far at all.

Things I Love about Riz

He never stopped moving.
The curly *c*'s of his hair.
The way his cheeks wobbled every step he took.

His laugh
     explosive
          unexpected
               invited you to come closer
                    like an unpopped bubble.

Muna Khala's Hands

When Amma naps,
my aunt Muna Khala
packs up two years of Rizwan
into five ugly boxes.

Keepsake Box

Muna Khala
brings us one box
that isn't ugly.

I like the way the lid
snaps shut,
a little click
the sound of hope.

Muna Khala tells
Aaliyah and me,
This box is for

cards
clothes
letters
memories . . .

Letters?

Sure . . .
Letters about Rizwan
or letters to Rizwan.

He's a very special person.
I like that Muna Khala
uses the present tense.

It feels like she's using it just for me.

Treats

Muna Khala takes us
out for Wendy's Frostys,
and gets us mediums
instead of smalls.

Even though the ice cream is
cold,
eating together
somewhere that's not home,
makes us feel
warm.

We feel special
until we see the little girl
the next booth over,
with two bows
      one red
      one blue
who is celebrating
turning three.

Her parents aim the camera.
How old are you today?

Threeeeeeeee!
she yells,
and has to use one hand
to hold down her fourth finger,
and her parents laugh.

I no longer feel warm.
We are looking at the three-year-old,
still looking,
until Aaliyah asks Muna Khala,
When will it stop hurting?
When will it hurt less?

Under the table
I reach for Aaliyah's hand.

And Muna Khala's face
droops,
drips
into her ice cream.
I don't know.
All we can do is pray
for strength.

Legacy

Amma nurses.
Amma rocks.
Amma sways.
She tells Nusaybah,
You have Aaliyah Api
Adnan Bhai
Rizwan Bhayya.

Whenever Amma
mentions Rizwan,
her eyes leak.
Amma sniffs big.
Her tears get small.
You have one big sister,
two big brothers.
One left early,
he went back to Allah.

They all love you very,
very much.

The sunlight streaming down on them
makes Amma glow.

Aqiqah Party

When Nusaybah was seven days old,
we did her aqiqah ceremony at home,
where Abu shaved Nusaybah's head
(then it grew back just like mine!)
and Nani Ami and Dadi
fed us lots of laddoos.

But today, Nusaybah is eight weeks old
and everyone is invited.

At the masjid
pink and purple balloons bob
but mostly pink.

The masjid smells like cinnamon,
and Sufian lays out trays of
sweet sugary circles.

He hands Aaliyah
a pink jar of sprinkles
and me
a purple jar of sprinkles.
Have fun!

Holding the jar
I sprinkle the tiny bits of sadness away.
It's nice to be in the masjid
when there are lots of smiles
instead of crying
and this time when people stare at me
my back doesn't feel hot
my shoulders don't slump.
Instead, I stand proudly
and watch my new little sister
take in the world.

Tiny Shadow

After we pray,
Imam Talha wraps me up
in a hug.
He holds Nusaybah like she's a loaf of bread.

Adnan, you have a new tiny shadow.
Assalamalaikum, Tiny Shadow!

Imam Talha hands me a tiny yellow bear
with black buttons for eyes

and a heart for a nose.
It's made out of the softest wool
I've ever touched before.

I made it for Nusaybah!

Nusaybah's Smile

Isn't as easy.
You have to work
to make her smile
but when she does smile
it's like sun peeping out of clouds
(so worth it).

Nusaybah's Hair

Matches mine
sticks right up
like lots of letter *l*'s.

Sufian says,
You know if you ever needed a broom,
you could just hold her upside down
and use her hair to sweep the floor.

Don't even think about it, Sufian!
yells Amma
while we laugh.

A Tiny Basketball

Sufian brings Nusaybah
a tiny foam basketball
painted in rainbow colors.
Nusaybah passes it from one hand to another
squeezes the ball

kicks it
drools on it too.

I think she likes it! says Sufian.

Some Days

Some days are just
like Nani Ami said they would be.
When it gets harder,
not easier.

And now and then,
a day gets easier.

Today Abu's at work.
Muna Khala is over,
telling us,
Go get dressed!
It's a beautiful day out!

Amma changes out of pajamas,
wears jeans,
a shirt with butterflies,

a light pink scarf
with crinkles
that remind me of potato chips.

Let's eat out!

Amma packs Nusaybah's rainbow basketball from
    Sufian
buckles Nusaybah in the car.
I put Riz's special shell in my pocket.
Aaliyah puts away her phone.
And off we go . . .

El Ranchero Restaurant

Amma
Muna Khala
Aaliyah
Nusaybah
and me.

Whenever Amma takes Nusaybah out of the car seat,
she stretches

for so long
looks like an upside-down question mark
Aaliyah giggles.
Muna Khala holds out her camera
takes a selfie,
but a family photo
without Riz
always feels like someone's
missing.

Amma takes the wrappers from our straws
twists them into paper hearts.
The waiter smiles,
takes our order.
It'll be right out.
He coos at Nusaybah,
looks directly at me.
Looks like you're
outnumbered.
What's it like
being the only boy?

Amma's smile fades.
Her fingers shred the paper hearts.
Her mouth closes into silence.
Even Nusaybah looks serious.

My fingers press into the baby-teeth ridges of Riz's
    shell.
I want Nusaybah to know,
I want her to remember.
I didn't use to be . . .
I wasn't the only boy.
Under the table
Aaliyah holds my hand.

The waiter's smile falters,
he puts down chips and salsa.
Enjoy.

When the waiter brings
steaming enchiladas,
sizzling shrimp,
and steamy bean burritos,
he avoids our eyes.

My stomach welcomes
the feeling of hunger,
the first time I've felt this way in a long time,
and the beans taste just as they should.
When the receipt comes,
Amma turns it to me
to show me the note
written by the numbers.

I'm sorry for your loss.

Amma sighs,
signs,
turns away,
starts to buckle Nusaybah
back in the car seat.

I pick up the pen,
roll it through my palms,
try to not write in chicken scratch

His name was Rizwan.

Abu's Question

In the family room
Abu stands by the table tennis table
Dani, do you want to play?
When I don't answer,
He tries again.
Adnan, do you want to play?

I'm playing with Nusaybah.

Abu nods
rubs his head.
Bring her here.

Nusaybah's eyes
no longer gray
brown now
grow big
when she sees Abu
toss the ball to her
and she holds out her squishy fingers
and leans as far as she can
to touch the ball.

Abu grins.
Look, Nusaybah! I have a magic trick!
Abu adds spin to the ball,
bouncing the ball back

Nusaybah's stomach wobbles
each time she giggles
makes us smile too.

Air Show Again

This year's air show
no one feels like going
without Riz.

Instead, we just stay home
are quieter than usual.
But the next day,
Abu cracks open the blinds
says I've found the perfect spot
Let's go.

Abu drives us to a playground
right next to the airport,
the DeKalb-Peachtree Airport Park Playground.

Airplanes take off
right next to bucket swings and curvy slides.

Nusaybah shrieks at planes
shrieks at swings
shrieks at everything.

Here, her smiles come easy!

Conversations of Cashiers

Amma
talks to everyone,
strangers like
cashiers,
delivery people,
neighbors.

The cashier admires Nusaybah.
Look at that spiky hair!
They grow up so fast.
Before you know it,
they're going to school
learning to drive,
and driving away from you.

Amma and I lift groceries into the cart,
Amma p a u s e s
looks back at the cashier.
Her face
moonlike
shining into a smile.
She's going to learn to swim too.

Leaving the Grocery Store

I see a little boy
who looks the same age as Riz.
Instead of looking away,
my hand moves in a wave
and he waves right back,
then looks and points up at the sky
at a soaring airplane.

I remember the four stages of flight—
    thrust
          weight
              drag
                    lift
and instead of feeling sadness,
right now
looking up at the plane
I feel lifted.

The ABCs of
Water Safety

Adult supervision
>   (Have a designated Water Watcher.)

Barrier
>   (Have a proper fence right by the pool without
>   big gaps.)

(The Florida pool had a fence
around the yard
but it had gaps—
a gap w   i   d   e   enough for a brother
to slip right through.)

Classes
>   (Teach your baby to survive in water.)

When Amma gets better
and can mention Riz's name
without crying,
she works with Dr. Olliver
to promote water safety.

Aaliyah and I help Amma assemble
        a list of infant swimming survival classes,
        pictures of pool safety alarms and fences,
        tips for families.

Aaliyah lines up the flyers
passes it to me
to press the stapler down.

I remember when I had a school project
needed to staple things.

Riz would press his hand on mine
whenever I would press the stapler down,
laugh at the click-click-clunk sound.

Even though I miss his fingers on mine
his hand on top of mine
(a mixture of sticky and soft)
I press the stapler down.
Keep on stapling.

It's the day before her presentation,
to a parent playgroup,
and Amma's eyes glaze over at the kitchen table.

Abu's hand circles Amma's back.
You don't have to do this.

It's just that
how can I talk about water safety,
when I couldn't even take care
of my own child?

Abu hugs Amma,
rests his chin on her bun.
The light of the lamp peeks through.
Amma looks up at him.
I know, but I have to.
I don't want anyone else to go through this.
Ever again.

Amma looks at Aaliyah and me.
Her eyes blink into a question
our nods an answer.

Swimmer Tots Academy

New blue building being built,
with big windows and trained instructors,
four exits away from our house.
Too late for Rizwan.
Not too late for Nusaybah.

Water Survival

Every week
for five days a week,
I tag along
while Amma drives twenty-two minutes
for Nusaybah's ten-minute swim class.

Amma tells me
> *I can drop you off at table tennis instead . . .*
> *if you want?*

I'm good.

Six weeks later
when Nusaybah turns nine months,
we sit by the pool,
holding our breath.

The swimming instructor
lets go.

Amma squeezes my hand
and Aaliyah's hand hard.
We squeeze back.
We watch as Nusaybah flips over
lifts herself onto her back
floats to the surface
cries.
Abu claps.
Aaliyah and I cheer.
This time Amma's tears are happy.

After Swim Class

I take Nusaybah,
tell her, *You did it, Nunu!*
I spike her wet hair
up into lots of letter *l*'s.
I lift her in my arms
like an airplane,
like I used to do
with Riz.
Nusaybah's stomach wobbles
and I can feel her laughing.

My arms
feel a little sad
but a lot happy too.

Courage

If Amma can
be brave
and get Nusaybah to swim.
Maybe I can
be brave
and get myself to play table tennis
again.

I remember the sound
the tap-tap
of the table tennis ball.

The sound of hope.

Nusaybah's Snuggles

Riz wouldn't put his head on our shoulders
except when he was tired.
Really tired.
And it felt extra special.

But Nusaybah puts her head
on our shoulders
snuggles in
all the time.

And it also feels extra special.

Sufian + Summar + Aaliyah + Nusaybah

Sufian, who always says what he thinks:
I really miss Riz
but Nusaybah is just SO cute.

You don't have to choose one,
says Aaliyah.

Summar spins Nusaybah around
while Aaliyah takes her
blows into her belly
making Nusaybah laugh each time.

Photo Session

Amma books family photos every year
the year before.

Amma almost cancels
but then decides that we still need photos,
says we are a family.

Our photographer, Katelyn,
meets us at Whittier Mill Park,
where the grass and fog and sun smush together.

Katelyn has hair the color of a fresh autumn leaf
and eyes the color of an old, smashed autumn leaf.

Amma brushed Nusaybah's hair flat
even added a bow
that matches Aaliyah's dress
but in a few minutes
Nusaybah's and my spiky hair reaches for the sky.

Behind her camera
Katelyn coos,

Y'all are perfect.
I've never met a baby as cute . . .
I think Nusaybah and Riz are tied.

Amma smiles a real smile
and Katelyn points out the red dot of lipstick on her
    front tooth,
which makes Amma giggle,
cover her hand with her mouth.

When the camera clicks,
we try again
look into the setting egg-yolk sun
and smile.

Easier Times

In Aaliyah's room
underneath her bulletin board,
I see the sad plant
that Sad Aunty gave us.
I thought I threw that away.
But it has no wilty leaves.
Instead, it has one perfect flower.

Aaliyah sees my stare,
snaps her fingers.
It needed a little love.

When There Is Sunlight

In my room
when the sunlight
is just so,
it glints off
my cracked trophy
and shines
on Riz's jellyfish.

In the Mailbox

There is a card
with writing—letters curling up.
The card is from a parent
who saw Amma's address
on a water safety brochure.

> *Because of your son,*
> *we repaired the fence to our pool.*
> *We even installed a pool safety alarm*
> *like you recommended that lets us know*
> *if anyone comes close.*
> *It saved our toddler's life.*
> *Thank you.*

Coach Khalil

Coach calls and texts
but up until now,
I didn't feel ready to answer.
I didn't feel ready to play.
This time when he texts,
I'm ready.

But first,
I walk over to the family room
run my hands over the table tennis table
take a deep breath
grab the paddle
walk over to Abu's room
knock-knock-knock
on the door.
Want to play?

Abu's Answer

Abu doesn't say anything
but immediately puts his papers down
clear his throat
pats me on the head
while his eyes get shiny.
Abu snaps his fingers
grabs his paddle
twirls it too.

I was waiting for you to ask . . .

Our Volleys

I'm a little bit rusty.
Okay . . .
Maybe a lot bit rusty.

Abu is too.

But each time
we tap the ball

back

        and

                forth.

We get a little bit

better.

At the Table

Coach Khalil
      leads me through stretches,
      tells me to breathe it out.
Coach Khalil
asks me how I am,
looks me in the eye
and waits.
When I say, *Better,*
he nods
picks up his paddle
says two of my favorite words:
      Let's play.

I want to say, *Good,*
but something about his look
makes the words spill out.

It's just—I still sometimes think
if I hadn't gone to the tournament,
hadn't gone to Florida,
Riz could still be with us.

Coach Khalil
shakes his head,
puts down his paddle.
It took me too long
to learn it wasn't my fault.
It's not your fault.

Got it?

I nod.
Got it.

I lift the paddle,
twirl it around,
drop it.

Okay, now see that, butterfingers?
Coach Khalil's lines on the sides of his eyes
deepen into a W.
He smiles.
That was your fault!

And I smile through my tears.

Nusaybah's Solids

I brought her something
Sufian pulls the foil off a tray
showing us sixteen lopsided squares
of Rice Krispie Treats.

I added extra butter
so it's soft for a baby!

Aaliyah giggles.
Are babies even allowed Rice Krispie Treats?

Abu says, *I don't see why not,*
but how about she finishes her khichri first?

After her khichri, Sufian holds out a Rice Krispie treat
and Nusaybah mashes it and puts a little in her mouth
then quickly grabs more.
Marshmallow cream coats her
cheeks
lips
chin
nose.
Sufian yells,
Just like Riz!

Rule of Thirds

In the sunny spot of the kitchen,
Amma mixes sugar,
melts butter,
coos to Nusaybah,
smiles as she licks a dollop of batter.

Are you okay having just the three of us?
I ask her.
I thought you wanted four, like four sticks of Kit Kat.

Amma stops the mixer,
looks right at me.
Oh, Dani,
it wasn't written for me.
but . . .
Amma pauses,
cracks an egg.

I also love Ferrero Rocher chocolates—
those come in threes.

There's something beautiful about three.
Have you heard about the rule of thirds in art?

Amma holds out three buttery fingers.

The rule of thirds:
Something about three is
pleasing to the eye,
like when you take photos,
or draw pictures
and divide it up in three parts,
they turn out to be . . .
stunning.

Hidden in the Pantry

Amma sees my face confused.
Hold on a sec . . .
This should make it clear.
Amma reaches an arm high
to pull down an old lunch box.
Don't tell anyone.
Here's my hidden chocolate stash.

In it gleams three golden spheres,
a pack of Ferrero Rocher chocolates.
See? Rocher chocolates come in threes.

Amma hands one to me
one to Aaliyah
and Nusaybah reaches for the crackling gold wrappers.

Too small for chocolate, Nunu!
How about I'll have your share?
Aaliyah has hers in one crunch
but Amma and I eat ours layer by layer
the nutty shell
then the chocolate wafer circle
then the gooey chocolate
then last of all the hazelnut in the middle.
Bliss.

Chocolate Frostys

Aaliyah likes dancing
but she's getting better at table tennis.

Aaliyah still doesn't care
whether she wins or loses
so I tell her
If you can get five points,
*I'll buy you a **large** chocolate Frosty.*

I notice Aaliyah is more consistent at hitting the ball
    back
smoothly and quickly.

She is getting closer—
this time she gets four.

At Wendy's I get Aaliyah
a large-sized chocolate Frosty
and give it to her as a surprise.
Aaliyah slurps and smiles.

My Favorite Thing

Smashing the ball down
on the very edge—
the corner of the table
is my favorite.
No opponent (especially Aaliyah) can get it
even if they tried.

My Favorite Sound

The tip-tap of the ball
back and forth
has a rhythm.

With Aaliyah
slow (her)
fast (me).

With Abu
(fast-fast).

With Amma
medium (her)
fast (me).

What I love—
changing up the rhythm.
just a little bit.

A Letter for the Keepsake Box

Even though my writing
is chicken scratch
I know Riz can read it.

I open up the notebook from Summar
uncap her pen
rip a page.

> Dear Rizzie,
> How are you?
> I miss you.
>
> I think of you
> whenever I see an airplane.
> I think of us.
>
> Did you know you're a big brother now?
> You have a little sister.
> But, no matter what,
> us men have to stick together,
> but also, us siblings too.

Love,
Adnan

(P.S. You're allowed to call me Dani.)

Table Tennis Tournament

I hear the sound
of the ball tapping.

The rhythm
invites me back.

I pick up my paddle.
The weight feels just right,
the ball nestled like an egg
deep in my palm.
I think
I'm ready
to play and win.

I lean into the serve,
watch the ball take flight—

And let go.

AUTHOR'S NOTE

My grandmother's cousin Yusuf died at two and a half years old.

> A day before Eid,
> in the flurry of Eid ironing,
> no one noticed.
> He was supposed to be napping
> but he wasn't.
> He climbed out of his crib
> wandered in the garden
> where the hose was,
> turned the water on,
> turned his life off.

Unfortunately, when it comes to drowning, it's the leading cause of accidental death for children one through four. Toddlers and infants need water safety. My hope is that we can teach our little ones to thrive not only on land but in the water too.

When I asked my ten-year-old what CPR was, she said, "CPR is what I learned about in PE. CPR is helping someone who is going to die." I thought that line was poignant and wove it into my manuscript.

Adnan's personality is inspired by my youngest brother. He is left-handed, color-blind, and plays table tennis in tournaments. I remember being dragged around to his table tennis tournaments as a child. Like Adnan and Aaliyah, my brother also says he'll buy me a chocolate milkshake if I get five or more points against him in table tennis. It hasn't happened . . . yet.

Like Adnan, I have a parent in the aviation field. My father works in the aviation field, and I found the four stages of flight fascinating. As a child, he taught me the aviation alphabet on a road trip, and I felt like it was our secret code.

"The water is not your friend!" is a line my cousin, a pediatrician, said to her toddler and preschooler daughters in the pool when they didn't follow directions and went further than they were supposed to in the pool. My cousin enrolled her daughters in ISR (Infant Swimming Resource) self-rescue classes. Five days a week, she would drive twenty minutes to take her daughters to their ten-minute class to learn to swim and survive in water. Purposefully avoiding floats, she guided her daughters in the water using the techniques she learned from the ISR classes. By teaching them that water isn't fun, she helped them learn safety strategies to survive in the water.

My hope is that Adnan's story inspires you and also alerts you to be vigilant about water safety, especially with our little ones.

My prayer is that our children thrive not only on land, but water . . . and air too.

RESOURCES

- www.drowningpreventionfoundation.org/resources
- Find an Infant Swimming Resource (ISR) Self-Rescue class near you: www.infantswim.com/instructor-locator.html.
- Centers for Disease Control and Prevention. "Drowning Prevention." www.cdc.gov/homeandrecreationalsafety/water-safety/index.html.
- Chillag, Amy. "Drowning is the leading cause of accidental death for your children. Here's how to prevent it." CNN Health, July 3, 2019, www.cnn.com/2019/07/03/health/iyw-drowning-prevention-trnd/index.html.
- The Sylas Project: www.thesylasproject.org.
- Learn more about the four stages of flight that help a plane soar: www.howthingsfly.si.edu/forces-flight/four-forces.

THE ABCS OF WATER SAFETY

Adult supervision
(Have a designated Water Watcher.)

Barrier
(Have a proper fence right by the pool
without big gaps.)

Classes
(Teach your baby to survive in water.)

If someone is missing, always check the water first.
Also, remove toys and floats from the water when you
are done swimming.

GLOSSARY

Abu: Urdu word for *father*

Allah: Arabic word for God

aloo: Urdu word for potato

Amma: Urdu word for *mother*

api: Urdu word for *big sister*

aqiqah: birth ceremony for Muslim babies that usually occurs at seven days

ayah: verse in the Quran

Bhai: Urdu word for addressing brother

Bhayya: Urdu word for addressing brother

biryani: spicy meat and rice cooked separately before being layered and cooked together

Bismillah: In the name of God (a Muslim prayer)

Dadi: paternal grandmother

duas: prayers

Eid: Muslim holiday

Fajr: Muslim prayer between dawn and sunrise

ghee: clarified butter made from the milk of a buffalo or cow and used in South Asian cooking.

haddi: bone

hadith: a record of the sayings of Prophet Muhammad

hijab: headscarf Muslim women or girls may wear

imam: mosque leader

Innalilahi wa innailahi rajioon: Verily to God do we belong and to God we return

inshallah: God willing

Janaza: Islamic burial prayer

juz: It's a book of the Quran. The Quran (the Muslim holy book) is separated into thirty sections.

Jumuah: Friday congregational prayer

keema: ground, spiced meat

Khala: maternal aunt

Khalu: uncle married to maternal aunt

kheer: milky dessert typically eaten on Eid and fancy occasions

khichri: rice and lentils cooked together until soft, cooked extra soft for babies

khutbah: sermon

kurta: Pakistani flowy shirt

laddoo: sweet, ball-shaped dessert popular in Pakistan, primarily made from flour, ghee, and sugar

Maghrib: Muslim prayer just after sunset

Mamu: Urdu word for *maternal uncle*

masjid: mosque or Muslim place of worship

Nana Abu: grandfather in Urdu; Abu means father

Nani: grandmother in Urdu

Nani Ami: grandmother in Urdu; Ami means mother

nihari: spicy stew with tender meat

pakora: spiced fritter

paratha: savory flat bread consisting of layers of cooked dough

Quran: Muslim holy book

Ramadan: ninth month of the Islamic calendar in which Muslims fast

sabrun jameela: Arabic phrase meaning *beautiful patience*, taken from the Quran

salam: peace; sometimes used as a greeting: *Salam!*

shalwar kameez: a traditional dress worn by women and men in Pakistan. The top, or kameez, is loose. The pants are usually wide on the legs but cuffed at the bottom.

Surah Mulk: a verse from the Quran that is recommended for Muslims to recite at bedtime

Theek hai?: Okay?

SUFIAN'S MANGO LASSI RECIPE

Ingredients:
    1 cup vanilla yogurt
    1 cup mango pulp
    1 cup ice

Blend together and enjoy!

ACKNOWLEDGMENTS

An enormous thank-you to:

Alyson Day and Eva Lynch-Comer for championing Adnan's story with passion and for believing in all my stories thus far! I appreciate it more than you can imagine.

Rena for believing in my voice and Adnan's, for your editorial insight, energy, and enthusiasm.

The dedicated Harper Team: Annabelle Sinoff, Nicole Moulaison, Shona McCarthy, Mark Rifkin, Molly Fehr, Joel Tippie, Karina Williams, Samantha Brown, Anna Bernard, Emma Meyer, and Emily Mannon.

Hazem Asif for the incredible illustrations.

My amazing SCBWI critique partners who are always there for me to offer encouragement during those rough drafts: Melissa Miles, Amy Board, Amber McBride, Vicki Wilson, Becky Sayler, and my first family readers: Khalajee, Amma, Anisa, and Zineera.

My WhatsaApp-Voice-Memo-Author Friends who help me boost my voice: Aya Khalil, Saadia Faruqi, Maleeha Siddiqui, Marzieh Abbas, and Nadine Presley.

BFFs Salma and Sarah.

My *entire* family in the United States, Pakistan, and beyond.

Amena and Asna for teaching me about Infant Swimming Resource classes and for being my favorite people to swim with.

Amma and Abba (Huma and Zaheer Faruqi) for taking care of me at all times, easy and hard.

Abajan, Mom, and Daado-Jan for your support.

Nana (Zarina Zakaria) for telling me Yusuf's story and inspiring me to tell Adnan's.

Hamzah, Talha, and Osman Faruqi, and Jim for table tennis inspiration.

Meymi and Mamujee (Zohair Zakaria)—for everything! Your names are in this book! ☺

My husband, Naoman, + Zineera, Anisa, Hanifa + New Baby for being who you are.

Devoted librarians, bloggers, authors, and educators for championing my stories and getting them into classrooms and into the hands of your students. Extra thank-you to Mrs. Ghazala Nizami, Dr. Gayatri Sethi, and my eleventh-grade English teacher, Mrs. Patricia Dobbs Carman.

Reader, thank you for picking up this book and for reading with me so far. I do so appreciate you and your kind reviews. I hope you'll stay with me for more.